ATLAS

EYE CANDY INK

SHAW HART

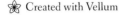

WANT A FREE BOOK?

*

She's a beautiful disaster and he can't walk away.

Atlas Warner is a god. With a needle in his hand, there's nothing he can't do. Except find pizza... and maybe love. The two things his life is currently lacking.

He's everything she ever deserved in life, but she refuses to see it.

With the body of a goddess, curves for days, and absolutely no sense of adventure, Darcy Rose doesn't have time for anything but work. Until Atlas barges into her life and refuses to let her fade into the background.

Together, they could have everything, if life doesn't tear them apart.

ONE

Atlas

MY BACK ACHES, the muscles tight and stiff from hours spent hunched over in uncomfortable positions. I roll my shoulders, trying to relieve some of the tension as I lean over Paul, my current client's calf, finishing the last of the shading on his new tattoo. His tattoo is a black pirate ship, the skull and crossbones flag flapping in the wind as it sinks into the sea. The design of the tattoo is simple enough, but what really makes it stand out is the coloring. The ocean is a watercolor design, done in cool shades of blue as it swallows up the sinking ship.

I let out the breath that I didn't realize I was holding as I grab the rag off my desk behind me and wipe away the excess ink, double-checking each line to make sure that every detail is perfect. I sit back in my chair, stretching my arms and back as I study it. When I'm satisfied that it's perfect, I grab the water bottle and some paper towels and clean off his calf so that he can get a clear view of his new ink.

"Shit, Atlas! You outdid yourself this time, man. That shit is sick, bro," Paul says.

I smile at him as I reach for my ointment and bandages. It's late, closing time, and I just want to dress and wrap his new ink and get him out the door so that I can head home and crash. Paul thanks me again as I snap off my latex gloves and hand him the aftercare instructions and walk him up front so that he can pay with Sam. I shake his hand and tell him to call me if there are any problems before I nod at Sam and head back to my room to clean up. She flips me off as I turn to leave, and I shake my head and try to hide my smile but I'm sure that she still saw.

Sam and I started at Eye Candy Ink about the same time. I had just finished my apprenticeship and was looking for a job, and she had just finished school. We ended up interviewing with Zeke, the owner of Eye Candy Ink, on the same day and we both got hired; Sam for the front counter and piercings and me as a tattoo artist. We both were right out of school and we're lucky that Zeke took a chance on us but we've proven our talent over the last two years and both of our careers have taken off. Moving to Pittsburgh for this job turned out to be the best thing to happen to me.

Sam was my first friend at the shop and in the city. We were both new to Pittsburgh, so we had bonded over exploring the city and finding our footing at Eye Candy Ink together. Luckily, everyone else who works at the shop was friendly too and we all clicked. I'm the youngest in the shop at twenty-four. Then there's Sam, Mischa, Nico, and the owner, Zeke.

Sam is like my older sister. She's a bit of a hardass, a true tomboy with a tough shell that's almost impossible to crack. She's slim and small, barely five-foot-three with silver eyes and a quarter sleeve on her right arm and several smaller ones on her back and hands. Her nose is pierced, and I'm sure she's got other things pierced, but I'll never ask. She dresses casually. In all of the time that I've known her, I've never seen her in anything other than jeans and T-shirts. She's not one of those girls who use fashion or her clothes as an art form. Instead, she uses her hair for that. She dyes it a different color every other week, matching it to her steadily growing collection of Converse sneakers. Right now, it's a bright neon purple and I know without looking that she has a pair of lilac high-top Converse on.

If Sam is the serious, tough girl, then Mischa is the exact opposite. He's a jokester, always wearing a smile and giving people shit or cracking jokes. He's got a similar coloring to me with dark hair, blue eyes, and pale skin, probably from spending most of our time inside at the shop. While my eyes are a pale icy blue, though, his are dark blue, almost black with a golden circle around the pupil. He's the same height as me, six-foot-three, with a similar thin, lanky build. He's got his nipples and lip pierced and is covered in tattoos, from his neck down to his toes. They're all black or gray and make him look even paler, but I have to admit, they're all well done and they do what he wants them to do, which is to hide his scars and keep most people away from him.

A lot of people are nervous when they see him walking down the street, but the truth is, Mischa wouldn't hurt a fly. He might not like to admit it, but he's a good guy. On the outside, he's a happy-go-lucky, laid-back guy who doesn't take life or anything too seriously, but as his roommate, I see more than everyone else. He's got a serious side and some stuff in his past that he doesn't like to talk about. I haven't pressed him for information but I can tell that whatever it is that happened, it still weighs on him.

He was the second person I met when I started working here, and he's a charismatic goofball that everyone loves, so we became fast friends. I had only just moved to Pittsburgh when I got this job and was looking for a roommate. Luckily for me, so was Mischa, and we've lived together for the past two years. He's a little messy and has a tendency to borrow my shirts when he forgets to do laundry, but he pays the rent on time and leaves me leftovers whenever he cooks.

Next, there's Nico. He's the big introvert in the shop. A giant at six-foot-eight and built like a linebacker with tattoos covering his neck and torso. I had been a little afraid of him when I first started, but it didn't take long to see that while he might look scary, with his almost permanent frown, tattoos, and size, he was actually a really gentle giant. A teddy bear, Sam calls him. With shaggy, chocolate brown hair and hazel eyes, he even kind of looks like a bear. He's been at Eye Candy Ink for close to a decade and he trained under Zeke. He's a good dude, super talented, but quiet and shy. In the two years that I've been at Eye Candy Ink, I think I've heard him say maybe a hundred words. He sticks to himself mostly, always doodling and drawing in one of his pads or listening to music. It was hard to get to know him since he rarely speaks but once he did, I realized that he's smart, sees far more than most people realize and he's loyal to a fault. He's also a kick-ass tattoo artist.

Last is Zeke, the owner of Eye Candy Ink, my boss, and a total artistic genius. At thirty-six, he's like the cool older brother that I never had and everyone in the shop's hero. He's six-foot-four and has light coloring and I swear he could pass for a Viking if he wanted to. Sam even tried to convince him to dress up as one last Halloween but he had refused. With wavy, chin-length, pale blonde hair and bright blue eyes, he reminds me of Ragnar Lothbrok from that *Vikings* TV show.

Dude is a legend. He's been doing tattoos since he bought his first tattoo gun from some sleazy pawn shop. He was fourteen at the time, and he taught himself how to tattoo, inking his friends or drunk people at parties. When he was eighteen, he started at some shitty tattoo parlor in Las Vegas. He bounced around Vegas and California for a couple of years before he moved to Pittsburgh when he turned twenty-six and decided to open his own place.

Eye Candy Ink opened its doors three months later. He built it from the ground up, hiring the best artists, and building the brand until it became well known for miles. Now it's the best tattoo shop in Pennsylvania, maybe even all of the East Coast. Zeke used to travel around tattooing celebrities and shit, but he's stopped doing that so much in the last six months. He's been sending Nico more often, and occasionally, Mischa or I have to go. None of us really like traveling like that though and I know that Zeke has turned some jobs down so that he doesn't have to ask us to go. Besides, we stay busy enough here that we don't really need to travel, especially now that Zeke's been cutting down the number of tattoos he does. He's been taking fewer and fewer clients for the last year or so and now he mainly just does the business side of things here. He'll still do tattoos for a select few clients but those are few and far between.

Zeke can do pretty much any tattoo style, but the rest of us tend to specialize in only one or two. Nico is a master at Japanese and tribal tattoos, basically any black work style. Mischa specializes in realistic and neo-traditional style, and I specialize in watercolor and new school. Sam can pierce anything and when she's not here, Nico fills in for her.

Over the last two years, these guys have become family. Well, like the family that I *wish* I had. My actual family is still back in Philadelphia and I get to see them a couple of times a year, usually for Christmas and someone's birthday. My parents are both lawyers and they always claim that they are too busy to bother calling me or making the trip. That's the excuse that I've heard all of my life. They missed my peewee soccer games because they had to work, they missed dinners and an art show that I did at school because of work. The job has always come first for them and I used to wonder why they even had me since they never seemed interested in spending time with me or really getting to know me.

I may look like my parents, with my dark midnight black hair and pale blue eyes, but that's where the similarities end. My mom and dad are more buttoned-up and I know that they don't understand my career or why I have so many tattoos and piercings. They were shocked when I came home with my first tattoo and pissed off when I had started gaging my ears. I had opted out of telling them about the nipple and cock piercings. Didn't want to give them a heart attack or anything. I thought that they were going to blow a gasket when I came home and told them that I had gotten an apprenticeship and was going to study to become a tattoo artist. I was eighteen by that time though and they couldn't do anything about it.

I had always loved to draw, and I think that they were hoping that I would be a graphic designer or something. Some kind of job that they saw as respectable. That's never been my style and I knew that if I stayed in Philadelphia that we would only go crazy with each other. It's not that they're really bad parents or anything. Maybe neglectful, but I know other kids had it far worse. They just don't understand me and if I'm honest, I don't understand them either. I only left Philadelphia because I didn't want to see the disappointment on their faces anymore or be disappointed in them when they missed another event or dinner because they got hung up at work. Even still, they are my parents and I feel some connection with them which is probably why I couldn't find it in me to move too far away from them. That was why I applied to jobs that were still close by, still in Pennsylvania.

They've always been serious and all about appearances. How they had a kid like me will always be a mystery. I've always been more of a dreamer, preferring to live in my head with my fantasies. I was a smart student but a pretty quiet kid, always doodling in my notebooks or on tests. I'm a bit of a softie, wearing my heart on my sleeve, and I know that I probably don't really fit the image that most people have in their heads when they picture a tattoo artist. I'm good though, really good, and Eye Candy Ink isn't exactly a dark and gritty tattoo shop. Maybe that's why I fit in so well here.

I head to the back of the shop to the office to grab some disinfectant wipes, nodding at Mischa as I pass by his room. He's still with a client, and I stop and lean my lanky frame against the wall to see what he's working on. It's a bright red origami bird and I grin at him when he looks up and wiggles his eyebrows at me. He and I always give each other shit about who is the better artist and I can already tell that he's going to be talking about this piece tomorrow.

The shop is converted from an old bar, with wood floors and dividers that make up each artist's room. A neon pink sign glows above the front of the shop, illuminating the dark night, and the shop logo is stenciled on the front window and door. I shake my head every time I see the name and I know that I would never have applied to work here if it wasn't for Zeke's reputation.

The waiting room is up front, right when you first walk in with the front desk, and a black wrought-iron gate separates that area from the back hallway and the artists' rooms. Binders filled with the tattoo artists designs are scattered on the end tables in the waiting area and more drawings are hanging on the walls. Mixed in with the tattoo designs are old photographs of Pittsburgh and some local artists' work that's for sale. A coat rack sits next to the front desk and chairs and a cool dark red, velvet, antique couch line the walls. The waiting area and hallway leading to the back are all painted the same royal turquoise color.

The front desk is made from old reclaimed wood with a computer, phone, printer, and credit card machine sitting on top. Stacks of Eye Candy Ink shirts, bumper stickers, and other merchandise for sale are hanging on the wall behind the desk with the different sizes and colors stacked up neatly underneath. A black leather office chair and a whiteboard with the work schedule and client list for the day pinned onto it completes the front desk area.

There are five artist rooms in total, and each is done up differently based on the artist who works in them. Mischa and I have rooms in the back of the shop, close to the back office, supply closet, and the bathrooms. Zeke's room is next to Mischa's, and Sam's piercing room is next to mine but neither of them uses the rooms on a daily basis. Up front, next to the waiting area and the front counter, is Nico's room.

Mine is painted a calming pale blue with tattoo drawings tacked up on two of the four walls. Framed posters of Van Gogh's *Starry Night* and Monet's *Water Lilies* hang on the wall, mixed in with my own personal designs.

I grab what I need from the supply closet, heading back to clean up my room before I head home for the night. I push some of my hair off of my forehead as I clean up my room, wiping down the chair, cleaning up the desk and ink, and taking care of my tattoo gun. I look around one last time before I close the door and start to head up front.

Mischa hears my door close, and I pause when I hear his chair wheel over toward me.

"Headed out?" he asks.

"Yeah, I'm going home to crash," I say, stifling a yawn.

"Were you going to pick up food on the way home?" he asks, his eyes widening to puppy dog level as he watches me.

"Pizza?" I ask with a smile at his antics.

"Perfect, man! Thanks."

I wave over my shoulder at him as I head toward the door, and I smile when he yells that he'll see me at home and calls me boo. I flip him off and grin when I hear him laugh and roll back into his room. His tattoo gun starts back up a second later and I push out through the wrought-iron gate and around to the front desk.

I lean against it and wait as Sam finishes typing something into the computer. She looks up at me, smiling as she reaches over to grab the envelope with my tips for the day in it.

"That pirate tat was rad, Atlas," she says as she passes me the envelope.

I pull the money out, counting it before I shove it into my pocket.

"Thanks, Sam. You all set to leave soon? I don't think that Mischa had that much left to do."

"Oh, yeah. I'm ready to head home," she says, rolling her shoulders back.

"You going to let Mischa walk you to your car tonight?" I ask her, giving her a hard stare across the desk.

I know she's tough and can take care of herself, but still, better safe than sorry. She leans back in her chair and rolls her eyes at me but nods and I smile, leaning over the counter before she can stop me and kissing the top of her head. I dance away quickly, barely escaping getting slapped as she lunges across the counter after me. I laugh and she flips me off as I push out the front door and head out into the night.

Since Mischa drove us to work, I'm stuck walking home, but luckily, we don't live too far from the shop. It's a nice night and I tip my head back, admiring the stars in the sky as I walk home. Our favorite pizza place is on the way and I stop in, picking up a large meat lovers with extra cheese before I head home.

We live on the third floor of this corner apartment building about eight blocks from the shop. It's not exactly fancy, but it's not falling apart either and it's safe, so that's good enough for us. Pittsburgh is an expensive city and while Mischa and I make more money working at Eye Candy Ink than any other shop here in the city, we're still not exactly millionaires.

Our place is two bedrooms and one bath with a combined kitchen and living room area. The floors throughout are a dark wood vinyl and the walls are pretty bare, probably because all of our drawings and artwork are at the shop. We have the usual leather couch and over-stuffed armchair that we got secondhand from my parents and a large flat-screen TV that we pooled our money and bought as soon as I moved in. Art supplies are scattered on the scuffed coffee table and some dirty dishes from this morning are sitting on an end table in the corner.

The kitchen has dark wood cabinets and a white countertop with black appliances. The kitchen appliances are a little older, but they all work, and honestly, we don't really cook that much anyway. The most I can make is spaghetti and cereal. Mischa can actually cook but with our hours at the shop, he doesn't do it that often.

A short hallway off the living room leads down to the bedrooms and bathroom. Mischa has the bigger room with a window that overlooks the main street. My room is a little smaller and overlooks the quieter street that leads toward the Ohio River and downtown. The bathroom sits between them, just a shower, toilet, and sink.

I'm finishing my second slice when the door opens and Mischa comes in, sighing as he tosses his keys on the counter and grabs his own slice of pizza. He inhales it in four bites and reaches for another and I shake my head at him.

"Dude, act like you've seen food before," I tease and he flips me off, polishing off his second slice just as fast as his first.

"Ugh, I'm too tired to deal with this. I'm going to bed. See you in the morning."

"Night. Thanks for grabbing the food, Atty."

"No problem," I say, covering my mouth as I yawn and head down the hallway to my bedroom.

I close the door, stripping off my clothes and falling face-first onto the mattress. My eyes close and I'm out as soon as my head hits the pillow.

TWO

Darcy

I DESPERATELY NEED A SHOWER.

My eyes flick over to the clock on the wall and I debate if I have enough time for a quick one before Indie, my best friend and roommate, gets home. I'm supposed to go with her to the tattoo place tonight and as my eyes catch sight of myself in the mirror, I decide that time doesn't matter. I've been working in the greenhouse all afternoon and I'm covered in dirt and God knows what else. I can't go anywhere looking like the sweaty mess that I am right now.

I strip quickly, tossing my dirty jeans and tank top in the hamper before I hop in the shower, soaping up and rinsing off as fast as I can. I squirt some body wash onto my shower poof and scrub at my skin, watching as the dirt swirls down the drain. I hate to wash my hair because I won't have enough time to blow dry it so I'll have to leave with it wet but that's probably better than going out in public with sweat-soaked strands sticking to my forehead and potting soil matted in the ends. Sighing, I pick up the shampoo and hurry through the rest of my shower.

I turn the water off and hurry to grab a towel. I know that Indie will be home any second and we don't have a lot of time before we have to leave to make it to her appointment on time. She's been waiting four months to get into this place so she can finally go get this tattoo and she'll kill me if we're late.

I told her she should just make an appointment at a different tattoo place, it's not like there aren't a hundred in this city, but she insisted on it being at Eye Candy Ink. They're supposed to be the best in the city and she said that if she was getting something tattooed on her skin permanently, that she wanted the best people to do it. I couldn't argue with that.

I step out of the shower and dry off, checking out my reflection in the mirror above the sink. My dirty blonde hair is a shade darker from the water and it's sticking to my face and dripping onto my shoulders. My hazel eyes are a bright honey color with forest green flecks dancing around the pupils. They're just a touch too large for my face and slanted down just a little at the edges. I run a critical eye over my round cheeks, flushed a bright pink from the heat of my shower, down over my nose, past my plump lips, to my chin. My face is just a little chubby, much like the rest of me, and I can feel my self-doubts start to creep in, so I hurry to turn away from my reflection. I'm just wrapping a towel around my body and stepping out of the bathroom when I hear the front door slam closed.

"Honey! I'm home!" Indie calls out and I roll my eyes.

She says the same thing almost every day and still thinks that she's funny. We've been best friends since third grade when she moved to Pittsburgh and was seated next to me in class. I was that quiet girl with the weird back brace that everyone thought was a freak and stayed away from but none of that seemed to bother Indie. She just plopped down in the chair next to me and started talking and she's barely stopped since.

Not that I mind. She was my only friend in school and she helped protect me from the bullies. I had scoliosis when I was younger and had to wear a back brace for a while. As if adolescence and high school wasn't rough enough, I had to do it with a giant metal brace around my torso. I got it off right before my senior year of high school but by then, the damage had been done. Everyone would always see me as "Back Brace Darcy", and I would always see them as bullies and assholes.

High school had been a nightmare but Indie and my grandparents had been there for me. I never knew my dad and my mom dropped me off with her parents when I was three and never came back. I found out later that she had died. An overdose, the police report said, in some pay-by-the-hour motel in Reno.

Luckily, my grandparents were still alive to take care of me. They worked hard to make sure that my medical bills were paid and that we had a roof over our heads and food on the table. They tried to protect me from the cruel things the kids at school said too and they treated me with kindness and made sure that I felt loved every single day. They were the best.

Indie and I moved in together after graduation. My grandparents had just passed and I was kind of lost. I had to deal with their funerals and selling their house. Indie had loved my grandparents too and I know that their deaths hit her hard too. She had helped me through every step of the way and we grieved and leaned on each other heavily. She's always been my biggest supporter and cheerleader, and I strive to be the same to her.

Indie is a computer programmer and she works at some giant tech company in downtown Pittsburgh. She designs software and helps people with IT at work and in her free time, she creates apps. She makes bank and her salary is the reason why we can afford this kick-ass apartment in downtown Pittsburgh so close to the river.

It's on the top floor in an apartment complex right along the Ohio River. A modern-styled place with copper and metal fixtures, exposed brick walls, and dark hardwood floors. The walls are all white and bare for the most part since Indie and I could never decide on a decorating scheme. We have a big kitchen with shiny stainless-steel appliances and marble countertops. A turquoise blue backsplash and white cabinets complete the look and make the whole room seem bright and relaxing.

Off the kitchen is the living room with a dark gray sectional and a black and white modern rug. A giant flatscreen TV hangs over the fireplace and on the opposite side, is an entire wall of windows, letting in light and a spectacular view of the river and city below. Indie's desk is set up next to the windows but she never sits there when she's working. She really just uses it to hold papers and to charge her laptop. If she's working, she sits on the sectional, leaning back against the soft cushions. More often than not she passes out there so we have extra blankets draped over the back of the couch.

Our rooms are down the hallway, one off to each side. Indie has the room overlooking the river and mine has the room overlooking the street. We each have our own bathrooms and walk-in closets. My room is painted a soft gray with a white canopy bed, navy comforter and sheets, and a gray dresser. A hamper sits in the corner of the room, over-flowing with clothes at the moment.

My bathroom is off to the right and the towels and bathmat are the same navy blue as my comforter and sheets. A shower curtain with different color waves and boats matches the rest of the color scheme. The vanity is gray with a white countertop, and all of the faucets and fixtures are stainless steel.

Indie's room is the only real spot of color in the whole apartment. It's painted a bright lavender color with a dark wood sleigh bed and neon pink comforter. She has a modern style dresser, dark wood with white drawers. Windows form one wall in the room with soft yellow curtains that she always seems to forget to close.

Her bathroom fixtures are the same as mine but that's where the similarities end. Where mine is done in blues, Indie's is bright like her bedroom. She has bright orange towels and a unicorn shower curtain. Somehow it works, and it suits Indie to a T.

My grandparents had left everything to me after they passed, not that they had much. It killed me to sell their house, but there was no way that I could afford the taxes and upkeep. With their savings and the house sale, I had just enough money to start my own company, a nursery and landscaping business.

I spent the first two years scraping by and barely able to make rent each month. Indie has never seemed to mind if I'm a little short on cash though. She was the one who supported and encouraged me to follow my dreams and start my nursery and after two years, I'm finally starting to see some success. I even had enough last year to expand the landscaping part of the business and I'm proud to say that my revenue is in the green now.

I got my love of plants and flowers from my grandma. We used to garden together all of the time and I learned everything I know from her. I know that she would be proud of me for following my dreams and doing something that we both enjoyed so much.

"Hey, I grabbed some sandwiches for us. Are you ready to go?" Indie asks as she walks around the corner and sees me brushing my hair in the mirror above my dresser.

"Yeah, just need to get dressed really quick."

"Hurry! The appointment is in twenty-five minutes."

"I'm going, I'm going," I tell her as I rush over to my closet and start to flip through clothes.

She follows after me and flops down onto my bed, almost rolling off the edge when the blanket slips. I laugh as I grab a T-shirt, bra, panties, and some cutoff jean shorts out of my closet. Normally I wouldn't wear anything so revealing but it's a heatwave out there today and I know that I'll be dying if I wear my usual baggy jeans and T-shirt.

I tug my clothes on quickly, trying not to stare at my too wide hips or the little roll of stomach that hangs over my shorts. The cellulite on my thighs catches my eye as I check out my reflection in the mirror on the back of my closet and I frown, turning away quickly. I'm dying to change but I know that if I do, we'll be late and I can't do that to Indie. I guess this outfit will have to do since I don't really have time to find something else.

"You look hot, Darcy!" Indie says as she somersaults off the bed.

I laugh at her and reach my hand out to grab her as she wobbles onto her feet and she grins back. I have no idea where she gets all of her energy from.

"I wish I had your body," I say, sighing as I take in Indie's pencil-thin legs and flat stomach.

She still has curves, just smaller, but she can pull off any outfit. If I didn't love her so much, I think I might hate her.

"I wish I had your curves. Guys go crazy over tits and ass like yours," she says with a wistful look at my body.

I roll my eyes but she ignores me, grabbing my hand and dragging me after her out into the kitchen. She tosses me a paper-wrapped sandwich and grabs her own off the kitchen counter before we both head for the front door. I barely have time to slip on my flip-flops and lock the door before Indie is dragging me down the hallway to the stairs. She takes my sandwich from me as I grab the hair tie off my wrist and tie my hair up into a messy bun on top of my head. She passes my sandwich back to me and unwraps her own as we hit the streets and head toward the tattoo shop.

Eye Candy Ink is only a couple of blocks over, so we decide to walk. It's still super hot but with the sun starting to set, it will be cool enough in no time. Indie is practically skipping as we head down the street and I try to pull her out of the way every time she almost bumps into someone.

"Why are you so excited? You know this is probably going to hurt, right?" I ask her.

"Don't remind me," she says, taking the last bite of her sandwich and tossing the wrapper into a nearby trash can. "You don't understand how crazy good this tattoo shop is. I'm just excited that I finally got into this place. Eye Candy has like a five-month waiting list! They're the best tattoo shop in the city, maybe even the state and everyone is always trying to get an appointment there."

I can see the pink neon sign glowing up ahead now and Indie claps her hands when she spots it. I finish my sandwich and toss the wrapper into the next trash can as the front of the shop comes into view.

"Besides, this place is supposed to be true to its name," she says, wiggling her eyebrows at me.

"What do you mean?"

"I mean, the guys who tattoo here are hot. Like drool-worthy, smoking, hot. So hot that it hurts to look at them directly," she gushes as she pulls the front door open.

"Sounds painful," I say dryly and she smacks my arm as I walk past her.

The guy behind the counter grins at me as I walk in and I realize that he heard the last part of our conversation. My eyes scan over him quickly and my steps falter.

Holy shit. Yes, the eye candy name really does fit. Fuck.

My cheeks heat and I look away from him. I turn and take in the front of the shop as Indie bounces up to the counter and checks in for her appointment. I pretend to check out some of the artwork on the walls as I listen to the guy's smooth, low voice as he checks Indie in.

"It will just be a couple of minutes," she says as she comes to take a seat in a chair in the corner.

I sit next to her on the crushed velvet antique sofa, picking up one of the binders next to me and starting to flip through it—anything to avoid looking back to the hot guy with the clear blue eyes and wavy black hair. His black T-shirt stretches across his chest and molds to his shoulders and biceps. Tattoos snake down both arms and cover his hands. My tongue darts out to lick my bottom lip as I wonder where else he has tattoos. I want to strip his shirt off and get a closer look at them, trace each one with my fingers and tongue. My mouth starts to water and I bite my lip as I shake my head to clear the wayward thoughts.

I peek back at him a moment later and blush when his light blue eyes meet mine. He gives me a friendly smile, a dimple popping out in his left cheek and I smile back weakly. I think he's going to say something but before he can, another guy opens the wrought-iron gate they have next to the desk and calls Indie's name.

This guy is hot just like the guy behind the counter and he actually looks a lot like him. *I wonder if they're brothers.* His hair is lighter and his eyes darker, but other than that, they could be twins. We follow him through the gate and down a short hallway and I walk closer to Indie, feeling the guy with the icy blue eyes watching me as I walk past him and out of his sight.

I breathe a sigh of relief when we step out of the hallway and into a smaller room. It's painted a dark forest green with drawings and artwork hanging everywhere. There's so much hanging on the walls that it's hard to figure out where to look first.

"Hey, I'm Mischa," the guy introduces himself and he holds his hand out to us.

"Indie and this is Darcy," Indie says, shaking his hand before I do the same.

"Nice to meet you both," Mischa says, smiling charmingly at us as he takes a seat in his chair and spins around to face the desk.

Indie's tattoo is already there on the top of the pile of paperwork, a blue outline on transparent paper. He picks it up and spins back around. I tune them out as they discuss the design and the best spot and placement for it. I step closer to one wall and take in some of the designs he has hanging there. They're all done in the same style for the most part and look like a classic tattoo. I wonder what style this is and suddenly, I wish that I knew more about tattoos.

This will be Indie's first one and she's been trying to talk me into getting one too. I already know what and where I would get it but I'm too chicken to make an appointment. I know that if I had to wait the four months that she did that I would talk myself out of it.

I walk closer to the door, checking out some of the tattoo designs hanging there and I'm startled when I hear a voice behind me.

"Is Mischa doing you too?"

I gasp and jerk my head in the direction of the doorway, my eyes widening when I see the guy from the front counter standing there. He leans against the doorframe next to me and I shift on my feet, looking over my shoulder at Indie and Mischa. It looks like they've got everything worked out because she's taking a seat in the chair and he's pulling on some black latex gloves.

"Uh, no. Just Indie today."

"You're not into tattoos?"

"No, I am."

"Do you have any?"

"No, not yet."

"Well, you're in the right place if you wanted to fix that."

His eyes stare into mine and I get lost for a minute as we watch each other.

"You want your friend to hold your hand?" I hear Mischa ask Indie behind me and I spin in my flip-flops to go to Indie, sitting in the chair next to the tattoo table and reaching out to hold her hand.

I squeeze her, giving her a reassuring smile as Mischa sanitizes Indie's lower arm and lays the outline down, making sure that it's situated perfectly. My nose burns slightly from the alcohol he used to clean her arm, and I scrunch my nose up, trying not to sneeze.

Indie's tattoo looks awesome and I know we both can't wait until it's done. She's getting a tattoo of a computer with some kind of code written on the screen. Red flowers wrap around the keyboard and up to bracket the screen. The black and red are going to look classic together. I lean forward to get a better look.

"Looks good?" Mischa asks her, holding up a mirror so she can check it out from another angle.

"Perfect," she says, grinning up at him.

He smirks at her, lining up capfuls of ink and preparing the tattoo machine and gun. We watch in silence as he puts a clean needle into the gun and she squeezes my hand when he spins around and grins at her.

"Ready?"

"Yeah, let's do this," Indie says, tensing when he turns the gun on and the loud buzz fills the room.

We both sit and watch the tattoo gun as Mischa leans in and starts to trace along the first line. She squeezes my hand as he continues the outline and I smile at her reassuringly, glancing away when I see a movement out of the corner of my eye. I turn and see that the guy from the front desk is still standing in the doorway watching me and I smile slightly at him, wondering why he's still hanging around. He smiles back and his dimple pops out again.

That's when I know that I'm in trouble.

THREE

Atlas

MISCHA WALKS up behind me to grab his next client and I stare after the two girls as they head back to his room. Jealousy courses through me and I send up a silent prayer that the curvy girl isn't the one he's tattooing. I glance at the clock, counting down the minutes until Sam comes back from her break and I can head back to his room to check on my girl.

I don't know what it is about her. Sure, she's got a banging body and the face of a goddess, but it's more than that. It was almost like being plugged into a current when my blue eyes meet her hazel ones. I never thought that I would fall for someone, let alone after just one look, but I can feel it in my bones. She's the one for me.

I think it was her sense of humor. I smile to myself as I remember the dry way she had responded to her friend when she described us as "so hot that it hurts to look at us." Most girls would have been excited to see us then, batting their eyelashes at us and trying to get our attention, but not this girl. She had seemed uninterested, barely looking at me when she first walked in. My eyes hadn't been able to look away from her though.

I'm used to chicks walking in here all dressed up, trying anything they can to get us to pay attention to them but my girl is dressed casually. I can't remember the last time I saw a girl without her hair perfectly styled and her face all made up. She doesn't need all of that to be beautiful anyway. She's gorgeous even in a loose tank and flip-flops, her hair still wet and barely a trace of makeup on her face. Her skin is tanned and I wonder what she does for a living. I can't wait to learn everything I can about her. I glance at the clock again, willing it to move faster.

Five more minutes.

I don't have another client for an hour and a half, so I've got time to go hang out in Mischa's room with my girl before I have to head to my room to get everything ready. I'm doing a butterfly on some chick later tonight and that won't take me long to draw up. Maybe I'll even have time to take her out for a quick bite to eat or a cup of coffee before I have to be back here.

I know the jokes that people say about Eye Candy Ink. So many people think that it's named because the people who work here are hot or that you have to be hot to work here. I wonder how shocked they'd be to find out that the name actually came about because Zeke lost a bet.

The front door opens and I'm out of my chair before Sam can even clear the threshold. She gives me a weird look and I grin at her, filling her in quickly on some of the phone calls I got before I try to walk as nonchalantly as I can back to Mischa's room. I lean against his open doorway and look around his room until my eyes land on my girl.

She's wandering around the small room, checking out the artwork and tattoo designs on the wall. Jealousy hits me and I look over to Mischa's desk, trying to see how many tattoo outlines he has on it. I don't think she is getting a tattoo because she didn't check in. I checked Mischa's schedule too when I was at the front counter but it just said one client for right now. Indie, six p.m., but I just need to be sure. His next appointment wasn't until eight-thirty p.m. and it was with a Rick so definitely not my girl.

"Is Mischa doing you too?" I ask, just to double-check, and I try not to smile when I see her jump and jerk her head in my direction.

I lean against the doorframe, staring back at her and trying to stop myself from reaching out and grabbing her. I want to grip her curvy hips in my hands, to feel her pressed up against me.

She looks away from me, back toward Mischa, and I almost growl. I don't want her looking at anyone but me and I'm about to say something else to get her attention when she answers me.

"Uh, no. Just Indie today."

Her voice is soft and melodic and my cock hardens in my jeans. I shift, trying to hide the bulge behind the doorway.

"You're not into tattoos?"

"No, I am."

"Do you have any?" I ask, my eyes scanning every inch of her bare skin that I can see.

"No, not yet."

"Well, you're in the right place if you wanted to fix that."

I stare into her eyes, grinning at her. My break is coming up soon and I'm starving but if she said she wanted a tattoo right now, I would skip it and take her back to my room. We could talk while I tattooed her and I'd ask her out on a date before I bandaged her up.

"You want your friend to hold your hand?" I hear Mischa ask and I glare at him over my girl's shoulder when she turns around to answer him.

He winces, giving me a 'sorry' look as my girl walks away from me, heading over to the chair in the corner of the room. She's tucked away in the far corner, sitting in the spare chair next to the tattoo table. I don't like that she's farther away from me now but there isn't really room for all of us in Mischa's room.

Her friend, Indie, I remember, is already on the table and I watch as Mischa transfers the tattoo stencil onto her arm. It's a pretty cool design and I watch as he carefully places it on her right arm. It starts at her wrist and ends halfway up her forearm and judging from the supplies on Mischa's desk, it's going to just be black and blood red. Shouldn't take that long then.

"Hey, Atlas. You need something, man?" Mischa asks when he looks up and sees me still leaning against his doorframe.

"Nah, I just don't have another appointment for a while. Thought I would hang out for a bit."

"That alright with you, Indie?" he asks, wanting to make sure that the client is comfortable with me hanging out in here while he's working on her.

"Fine with me."

She smiles at Mischa as they discuss the design one last time and my eyes find their way back to my girl. She's looking around the room again, her legs tucked underneath her chair and her fingers twisting together in her lap.

"So, no tattoo for you today then, huh?" I ask her and she smiles slightly at me.

"Me? No, I'm just here for support," she says, motioning with one hand to Indie.

"Good friend," I say and she blushes slightly.

God, this girl is so sweet. Maybe that's why I'm so into her. Most girls that come in here are forward, aggressive flirts. Hell, some of the girls I don't think even want tattoos, just a reason to get close to us. My girl doesn't seem like that at all. She hasn't made goo-goo eyes at me once and she seems to genuinely just be here to support her friend. My eyes narrow. I wonder if she's only acting like this because she has a thing for Mischa instead but as I watch her, I notice that she barely looks at him either.

"You can get a tattoo now if you want. I'll be fine," Indie says to my girl.

"No, I said I'd be here for you."

"Did you already have an idea or something in mind that you wanted?"

"Yeah," she admits, her eyes flicking over to her friend as Mischa turns on his tattoo gun.

My ears perk up at this and I'm already picturing her spread out on my tattoo table. I smile when she reaches her hand out to her friend, letting her squeeze her fingers as Mischa starts to work.

"What did you want done?" I ask after a minute, moving closer to her chair in the corner and leaning against the wall so we can talk over the noise.

"Oh, um, a flower, running along my spine."

"That spot will hurt," I warn her.

"It has to be there," she says and I notice that Indie shoots a glance at her.

I tuck that information away, determined to find out later why it has to be there.

"What kind of flower? Something detailed? What about colors? Or did you want it just to be black?" I shoot off questions at her and her eyes widen slightly.

"I was thinking something minimalist looking but still pretty. Just black, or maybe a gray? With red or maybe a watercolor design on the petals."

I grin at the watercolor part. My specialty, which means that it would make sense for her to book with me. Thank god. I know that she'll have to take her bra and shirt off to get that done and I don't know what I would do if she were topless with someone else. Jealousy floods my body as I picture some other guy seeing her like that and I grit my teeth, trying to shake the image from my head.

"I can do it for you. I'm the best at watercolor in the shop," I boast and I glare at Mischa when I see him grinning at me.

"Oh, that's really nice of you, but I wasn't planning on getting anything done today. Maybe I'll make an appointment at the front desk when we leave."

Yeah, and then I won't see her for months.

"I'm Atlas, by the way," I say as I offer her my hand.

"Darcy," she says quietly, her smaller hand slipping into mine and squeezing slightly as she shakes my hand.

Her hand fits in mine perfectly. Her fingers are calloused, and I wonder what she does for a living. Before I can ask though, Sam calls out to me.

"Hey, Atlas! I've got a client. Think you can watch the front counter for a little bit?"

I growl under my breath, upset that I have to leave my girl right when she was starting to open up to me but I know that everyone else in the shop is with a client.

"Yeah, no problem," I call back to her.

"Let me know if you want that tattoo done," I say, pointing at Darcy as I back out of the room.

She gives me a small smile and a nod and I see Mischa looking at me strangely, like I have two heads as I start to back out of the room. I know that I'm acting weird. I've never shown an interest in any girl before and now I'm all over this one. I smile at Darcy one last time before I turn and head down the hall to take over for Sam. As I leave his room and slip behind the counter, I try to ignore Mischa's watchful eyes.

"Thanks," Sam says as she leads her client, a nervous looking girl back to her room.

I keep one eye on the front door and one on Mischa's room for the next half hour. I know that Mischa still had quite a bit to do, so it's not like Darcy will be leaving anytime soon but I'm still anxious.

I need to get her number or secure something, a date or an appointment with her, so that I can see her again. I bite my lip as I take out my pad and start to sketch the tattoo that she described.

FOUR

Darcy

INDIE IS ALMOST DONE with her tattoo and as Mischa
wipes it off and starts to bandage it up, I excuse myself to
the bathroom.

"Yeah, it's just down the hallway there. Third door on
the left," he says, pointing out the doorway and to the right.

"Thanks," I say, squeezing past the table and out the
door.

I glance toward the front of the shop, my eyes meeting
Atlas's quickly before I look away and head in the opposite
direction. I walk quickly down the short hallway, slowing to
admire some of the designs and artwork covering the walls.

I find the bathroom and sneak inside, taking care of
business before I wash my hands, leaning on the sink after
and staring at my reflection in the mirror. I study my face,
taking in my too-large eyes and the bump in my nose from
where I broke it when I was twelve. My bottom lip is
slightly bigger than my top and my chin is just a bit too

pointed. My hair is just now drying and some pieces have come loose from my bun, curling against the back of my neck. I look like a mess.

I take my hair down, shaking it out and let out a sigh. It almost seemed like that Atlas guy was flirting with me but that can't be right. The guy looks like a Greek god with his sculpted cheekbones and jawline that looks like it could cut glass. He could get any girl he wanted. He's some badass hottie with tattoos and cool hair and a gorgeous face and body and I'm just, well... me. I turn away from the mirror, growing disgusted with my reflection and the hope that had started that I could get a guy like that.

He was just being friendly. He's probably just nice to everyone. He can get some more clients that way I'm sure. I try to convince myself that he was just being polite and not to read anything into it but I can't deny the way my heart flipped over in my chest at the idea that he could be interested in me. I shake my head, trying to clear my foolish thoughts and open the bathroom door. I need to get back to Indie or she's going to get worried about me.

I barely make it two steps out into the hallway before Atlas is there, his hands on my waist as he pushes me back against the wall. *Was he waiting for me?* I gawk up at him, meeting his eyes that are locked on my face as his fingers brush under my shirt and run along my hips. His fingers tickle me there and I wiggle slightly in his hold.

He steps closer into me and I breathe in his scent, my eyelashes fluttering as he presses against me. He smells like wood and disinfectant and it should smell terrible but on him, it works. Or it works for me anyway. I press my thighs together, tipping my head back and looking into his clear blue eyes.

I don't know what it is about him. He's so intense and

focused on me and I've never had anyone treat me like this. He can't seem to tear his eyes away from me and it's a little unnerving. He reaches up with one hand, his long fingers brushing away some of my hair that fell forward from my face. His eyes seem mesmerized by it and I watch as he rubs the strand between his fingers before he gently tucks it behind my ear. His eyes meet mine again as he towers over me.

"If you want a tattoo, you come to me," he says quietly as he leans impossibly closer to me.

His minty breath washes over my face and distracts me from his words. My eyes stray to his mouth, taking in the shape of his lips, the shade of red they are. I nervously bite my bottom lip as I study his mouth. His tongue runs along his full bottom lip and I almost moan at the sight, wishing that his tongue was running against me instead. I shake my head, trying to get my body under control.

"What?" I ask, confused about what the heck is going on.

I lick my suddenly dry lips and blink up at him. His eyes catch the movement and I watch his pupils dilate as he stares at my mouth. My lips start to tingle from his gaze and I shift, rubbing against him slightly. That seems to snap him out of it and his eyes meet mine once again, the light blue turning a little cloudy as my body brushes against him.

"If you want a tattoo, you come to me," he says, his voice deeper, more forceful this time.

"Why?" I ask.

Surely, he can't be that hard up for clients. Indie said this place had a crazy long waitlist and after seeing the artwork hanging up all over the place, I can see why. Why is he so adamant that I come to him for all of my tattoo needs?

"No one can do you better than me."

My mouth drops open at his words and I can feel my face flame with heat at the way I could take his words. I'm sure my cheeks are fire engine red right now. *Great. He just meant the tattoo, Darcy. Get your mind out of the gutter.*

"Okay, sure," I whisper back, trying to get my face to cool off. My eyes glance down the hall to Mischa's room and I wonder how weird it would look if I just shoved him and took off running down the hallway.

"I mean it, Darcy. No one else touches you. No one else tattoos this gorgeous body. Just me."

My gaze snaps back to him and I stare up into his eyes, seeing that he is dead serious and I can only nod at him. I don't know why he's so insistent on this but I'm not going to argue with him.

"Say it, Darcy. Promise me that no one else inks you, no one else touches you."

"Okay," I agree. "I promise. Only you."

His eyes darken and I wonder what mine look like as I stare back at him. I get tunnel vision, lost in his eyes, in the feel of his hands on me, his body pressing against mine until everything else just seems to fade away. We watch each other and it's like I'm frozen in place, trapped in his heated gaze as nerves and excitement course through my blood. I should leave, snap out of it because there's no way this ends well for me but I can't. I'm too curious to see what he'll do next.

His eyes flick to my mouth again and he licks his lips. I let out a shaky breath as his head leans down toward me and I arch up toward him, desperate to feel his mouth on mine. Laughter and loud voices break through the fog and I blink hard, forcing myself back to reality. *What the heck am I doing? This isn't me. I don't go around kissing guys that I just met. Hell, I don't kiss guys at all!*

This guy has heartbreak written all over him and I panic when I see Indie and Mischa start to walk out of his room out of the corner of my eye. Before Atlas can get any closer to me, I duck under his arm and practically sprint away from him.

Indie gives me a curious look when I get to them and I smile at her shakily. I'm sure I look crazy, breathing hard, my face flushed and eyes dark with emotions. I see her eyes dart behind me and I know that Atlas is still there. I can feel his eyes locked on me and I hear his footsteps get closer, trailing after me. As we follow Mischa up to the front desk to pay, I grabbed Indie's hand and pulled her along with me.

The metal gate closes behind me with a loud clunk and I let out a sigh, knowing that Atlas is on the other side of it. I have a feeling that I'm going to need something more than a gate between us to keep me from jumping him though. He's too potent, too attractive, and his attention must just be a game. I had guys in high school pretend to be interested in me only for it to be some hurtful joke. I don't get that feeling from Atlas but I've been wrong in the past.

I keep my eyes locked on the ground as Mischa waits until the girl sitting there now gets off the phone before he says goodbye to us. My eyes itch, burning to take one last look at Atlas but I keep them away from the hallway. I know he's over there. I can feel his gaze on me like a caress and I know that he's standing just to the side of the front desk.

"It was nice to meet you both. Sam here will check you out, okay Indie?" Mischa says as he nods to the girl behind the counter.

"Yeah, thanks again. I love it!" she says, throwing her arms around him in a quick hug.

Mischa seems taken by surprise for a second but then I

watch as his eyes soften and he hugs her back slowly. I'm not surprised; everyone loves Indie. He pats her awkwardly on the back once. His movements seem rusty, like he's not used to people touching him and I wonder about that for a second.

I refrain from hugging him and wave at him instead. He smiles crookedly and waves back at me before he unlatches the gate and heads back down the hallway to his room. I wait next to Indie as she pays, doing my best not to look back toward where I know Atlas is standing. I blush as I finally give in to the urge and look up.

Mischa and Atlas are both standing there, leaning against the wall next to the front counter. Misha has a weird expression on his face as he watches Indie, smiling softly when she says something to Sam, and they both laugh. I glance away from him to Atlas and see that his eyes are still locked on me.

Indie finishes paying and stuffs her wallet back in her purse as I continue to have my staring contest with Atlas. He gives me a heated look and I nod slightly at him before I grab Indie's hand and drag her out of there.

FIVE

Atlas

IT'S BEEN three days since I watched Darcy walk out the door. I've been watching the front desk, straining to hear if Sam ever talks to my girl, but so far, nothing. I'm sure I don't have to try that hard. Everyone in the shop knows how I feel about Darcy and I know that if she called, Sam would tell me right away.

She and the guys have been giving me a hard time ever since she left. I should have known that Mischa wouldn't be able to keep his mouth shut. He's been ribbing me non-stop about my crush on Darcy and how strange I had been acting. The entire drive home after she left, he had been trying to give me tips on picking up girls and he's been sending me articles on how to talk to them ever since. I just roll my eyes at each one.

I know that I came on a little strong but I couldn't seem to help myself. What was I supposed to do when I met my future wife? Well, the answer is to get her last name or phone number before she slips through your fingers.

Last night, Zeke, Mischa, and I had been closing down the shop and all I heard were jokes about my flirting and pick-up skills. Mischa said maybe I shouldn't be allowed to work at Eye Candy Ink and joked that I wasn't hot enough while he fluffed his hair in the mirror next to the back office, batting his eyes at me as he made a duck face with his mouth. Zeke had laughed and they had started joking about who was the hottest. Mischa said I was last and I had to remind him that we looked like twins. All of this because Darcy couldn't seem to get away from me fast enough.

Everyone who works at Eye Candy Ink seems to be anti-relationship. I never really got the full story on the rest of the guys, but I know that Mischa had some family issues and so he tends to stick to one-night stands. Although he hasn't been with anyone for a while. I wonder if he's ready to get past everything and be in a relationship. My mind flashes back and I remember the way that he had been looking at Indie and visions of us on double dates fill my head.

Relationships have never been an interest for me either but I'm not against them like everyone else. My one and only relationship was in high school and I was only with her because her parents were friends with mine and I was trying to make them happy. She had cheated on me and I had ended things and that was that. I've been single ever since but not because I hate relationships and love like everyone else seems to. I've just never met anyone who has made me want to settle down. Not until Darcy.

I'm back at the shop now, all of us hanging out in the front before we officially open. Nico is sitting in a chair in the waiting area, reading a magazine and just generally keeping to himself. As usual. Mischa paces back and forth in front of him, unable to sit still for longer than a few minutes. I lean against the front counter, staring out the window at the people who pass by. Sam and Zeke are behind the counter looking over some computer software that we got for scheduling that's been acting up. They both look annoyed and I glare at the computer. The scheduling software that we just got somehow malfunctioned and erased the last three months of appointments. I'm the one who figured that out after I tried to find Indie's contact information so that I could get in touch with Darcy. I watch as Sam pulls on the ends of her hair, a sure sign that she's annoyed and frustrated. Zeke runs his hands through his own hair and lets out a sigh.

"Too bad Atlas ran off that girl. Her friend is a computer programmer. Bet she could have had it up and running in no time," Mischa says as he paces over to the far wall and starts messing with some of the tattoo designs that are tacked up there. He rearranges some, making sure that all are clearly visible, their edges neat before he backs up and starts pacing again. I roll my eyes at his teasing and he grins at me before he turns and sprawls out in the chair next to Nico.

"You should have seen it, Nico. Atlas was trying his best to hit on her and just ended up scaring her away. The look on his face when she ran out of here was priceless."

Nico rolls his eyes at Mischa's story, shifting in his chair and ignoring him as he flips through another page in his tattoo magazine.

"Did you get Indie's number? I saw the way you were looking at her," I cut in and Mischa's cheeks turn pink.

"What would I want with her number? Not like I'm

going to call her or try to date her," he says, pushing to his feet and pacing back and forth again.

Nico tucks his feet under his chair, moving them out of the way of Mischa as he starts to wander around.

"You let her *hug* you."

Everyone freezes and we all turn to stare at him. Mischa is weird about physical touching. He never lets anyone get close to him. I've seen hundreds of girls try to hug him or kiss him goodbye and he always ducks out of the way before they can touch him.

"What!?!" Sam says, a gleeful smile on her face.

"Yeah, this is WAY more interesting than Atlas and Darcy," Zeke says as he leans against the front counter next to the computer.

Nico doesn't say anything but he's stopped reading his magazine and I can see him watching Mischa, a curious look on his face. I wonder what he sees. For someone who never seems that interested in others, Nico always seems to have more insight then you would expect.

Mischa crosses his arms over his chest, glaring at all of us in turn before he turns and paces back to the wall.

"She just caught me off guard. Girl moved quick," he says, sounding annoyed.

His cheeks are still pink though and I wonder if that's really the truth. Before I can say anything else on the subject though, he brings it back to Darcy and me.

"We were talking about Atlas and how his one true love is never coming back."

He spits the one true love part out between clenched teeth and I decide to let him off the hook.

"Don't listen to him. She'll be back," I say, trying to convey confidence.

Mischa grins at me and I can see the relief that we let

him and Indie go in his eyes. I nod at him, pushing through the gate as I head back to my room. Sam will be unlocking the doors any minute and I'm booked for most of the day. I straighten everything on my workspace, making sure that everything is stocked and I have the tattoos that I'm doing today done and ready to go.

Tomorrow is one of my days off and I make a mental checklist of all of the errands that I need to run. Maybe I could do some light Instagram stalking and find Darcy. How many Darcys in Pittsburgh could there really be? A lot, apparently. I've already checked Facebook and Twitter and she must have a private account or none at all because I couldn't find her on there. If I could just find her somehow, then I could message her and make plans for her tattoo, or maybe we could grab dinner or drinks.

My mind flashes back to Darcy for the millionth time in the last three days and I sigh as I lean back in my seat. She had been into me. I remember the way her pupils had dilated when I had stopped her outside the bathroom. She promised me that no one else would tattoo her and I trust her, but that doesn't mean that she's going to get a tattoo right now. Can I wait for her to be ready? For her to come back to me? No, I don't think I can. I know deep in my bones that Darcy is the one for me.

The problem is that Darcy had seemed so shy, so timid, and I don't know if she will be back or not. She had been into me but I got the impression that she wasn't the type to flirt or go after some guy. I hope I'm wrong because I don't know what I'll do if I can't find her. Watching her walk away felt like the biggest mistake of my life.

The front door jingles and I blink back to the present, getting everything laid out before I go to greet my first client.

SIX

Darcy

I GROAN as I hit the backspace on my computer for the third time in the last fifteen minutes. I'm sitting in my cramped office at the back of the nursery building working on finishing up payroll, or trying to anyway. Atlas keeps sneaking into my thoughts.

I rest my elbows on my old scarred desk, leaning back in my office chair as I try once again to push him from my thoughts. I don't know what it is about him. Maybe how he looked or the way that he talked to me but that doesn't seem true. I've seen hot guys before and haven't been affected. I've never had someone talk to me like that though. So... dominant, and sure of himself.

I've woken up with soaking wet panties the last six mornings after having dreams about what would have happened if I hadn't run away from him. In my fantasies, he kisses me, holds me against the wall and keeps me there with his body pressed against mine. Our tongues tangle together as his erection shifts and fits between my thighs. I wish that I had let him kiss me. I wish that I would have touched him back, felt how hard and strong his body was under my fingertips.

I try to clear my head and focus back on the computer screen. If I let that fantasy play out then I'm going to need to change my panties again and I don't keep a spare pair here with me at work.

The door to my office opens and I startle in my chair, letting out a sigh and rubbing my eyes when I see Indie skip into my tiny office. She plops down in the single chair across from me and I already know what she's going to say before she opens her mouth.

She's been on me to go back and see Atlas ever since we left Eye Candy Ink. She wants me to take him up on his offer for a tattoo and on anything else that he might want to give me. I blush just thinking about doing that and I see Indie grin at me, her straight white teeth gleaming in the lamplight.

"Thinking about your man again? I don't blame you. I'd be blushing if I had a guy as hot as Atlas panting after me."

"He's not my guy and he's not panting after me," I correct her but she just shakes her head at me.

"He's totally into you. He's probably waiting on your call right now. I bet he's been crying himself to sleep every night since you walked away."

I giggle at that. I can't see a tough guy like Atlas crying over anything.

"I think that you should go see him, Darcy. Call and make an appointment or maybe just show up? What do you have to lose? Besides your V card?"

"Why would a guy like that be into me," I mumble before I can stop myself.

My face flames hot and I know that Indie heard me. She looks so sad for a moment and I open my mouth to say something, what, I don't know, but she beats me to it.

"You're so beautiful, Darcy and I don't even think that you realize that. Guys check you out all of the time. When are you going to see yourself the way everyone else does?"

I stare down at my lap and she continues, softer now.

"You're not that girl in high school anymore. The brace is gone, Darcy. You don't need to let what people said back then influence how you see yourself now."

"I still feel like that girl," I whisper and I see Indie's expression fall.

"I wish you wouldn't let them control you like this. They're gone. We're going to go back for a high school reunion in a few years and you're going to see that everyone that put you down is a huge loser now. Meanwhile, you're successful and strong and so dang pretty. All our dumb old classmates are going to be so embarrassed that they ever said a bad word about you."

"You have to say that. You're my best friend."

"Nah, best friends are honest with each other. I'm telling you the truth, Darcy. You were awesome back then. Those kids were just young and dumb. That's why they couldn't see how amazing you are. Me? I've always been smarter than everyone else which is why I was able to recognize how incredible you are."

I giggle as she kicks her feet up on my desk and almost tips over backward in her chair. She laughs at herself and drops her feet safely back to the floor. Her face sobers after a minute though and she watches me across the desk.

"Guys are dying to find a girl as cool as you, Darcy, and Atlas seems to be the first one to catch your eye in return. I think you should give him a chance. Just promise me you'll think about it, okay? It's time that you started seeing your-self for who you really are. You're drop-dead gorgeous and stronger than you realize."

I nod my head at her, wiping a few stray tears from under my eye. She smiles softly at me as I get myself together. I don't know what I would do if I didn't have Indie.

"I love you, best friend."

"I love you too, best friend," I say and she grins as she jumps out of her chair and comes around my desk to hug me.

My elbow bounces off the desk and hers hits the wall in the tight space but we laugh together and make do. I don't know what I did to deserve her but I'm so happy that she's here with me, that I get to go through life with her by my side.

I think about her words as I close down the office and we head back to the apartment and when we curl up on the couch together to watch old *Friends* reruns and eat maca-roni and cheese. By the time that we both fall asleep on the couch together, I've already made up my mind.

I'm going to get a tattoo.

SEVEN

Atlas

IT'S BEEN ten days since Darcy walked out of the shop and any hope that I had that she would be back has dwindled to nothing. I tried fixing the software and looking through any of the paperwork for Indie's information but I couldn't find anything. I've tried finding her on social media, but without a last name, I haven't had much luck. It feels like I'm losing my mind without her and I wonder how someone that I only spent half an hour with could leave such a lasting impression on me.

I've been kicking myself all week, wishing that I had gotten her phone number or made an appointment with her right then and there. Then at least I could have known that I was going to see her again. I've been having trouble concentrating the last couple of days and I know that it's because of Darcy. I need to figure out a way to see her again, to ask her out on a date.

Today is Sam's day off, so I'm helping to cover the front

desk with Zeke. He's in the back doing paperwork right now but my next client should be here soon and I know he'll be making his way up here to take over for me.

The phone rings on the counter and I rub my forehead, trying to ease the headache that's starting to build behind my eyes as I reach forward to answer it.

"Eye Candy Ink," I say, my voice void of emotion.

"Um... hi, I was in a few days ago with my friend and I wanted to schedule an appointment."

The voice on the other end of the line sounds timid but familiar and my heart starts to race as I begin to hope that it's Darcy.

"Sure, what's your name?"

"Um, Darcy. Darcy Rose. I was in with my friend Indie and—"

"I remember you. This is Atlas," I say, grinning like a lunatic. "I'm really glad you called, Darcy."

"You are?"

"Yeah," I say, my grin stretching even wider across my face. "Let me pull up my schedule really quick. When did you want to come in?"

"Well, I work every day but I get off at six p.m. I know Indie said that you guys are booked like months in advance."

"Okay, no problem. I'm sure I can fit you in sooner."

Even if I have to cancel someone else's appointment, I think as I click through my schedule on the computer. I start to flip through my calendar and realize that she's right. My days are booked for the next three months. I bite my bottom lip, worrying it between my teeth as I try to think. I can't wait three months to see my girl again.

"Yeah, I'm booked for the next three months but I can always fit you in after hours. The tattoo I have in mind won't take long to do. It will be minimalist like you wanted and since most of it is black, it should only take about an hour. We close at nine p.m. so I can fit you in after that, if that works?"

"Are you sure that's okay?" she asks and I can practically see her twisting her fingers together.

"I'm positive. What day did you want to come in?"

My mind is already coming up with fantasies of the two of us alone in the shop and my cock gets hard, pressing against the zipper of my jeans.

"Does Tuesday night work for you?" she asks and I blink back to reality, clearing my throat as I bring up the schedule and check that my last appointment will be done by nine p.m.

"Yeah, Tuesday is perfect."

I enter her name into the system and get her phone number next, typing that into the computer and then saving it into my phone too. Can't have the system messing up and losing her info again.

"I have an idea in mind but if you can send me any pictures or descriptions of what you wanted that would help too. I can text you what I have drawn up too."

"Okay, I'll try to find some pictures. I'd love to see what you already came up with too though."

"No problem, I'll send you some pictures in a little bit."

"Cool. Thanks for doing this, Atlas," she says and I feel my cock harden at the sound of my name coming from her lips. Lips that I'm dying to feel against mine.

"Anything for you, Darcy."

She pauses at that and I grin like a lunatic.

"See you Tuesday," she says and we end the call a second later.

I spin around in my chair, throwing my hands over my head and I hear a chuckle behind me.

"Let me guess, that girl you've been crushing on finally called," Zeke says as he comes to take over for me at the front counter.

"Yeah, she's coming in on Tuesday at nine p.m. Is it okay for me to stay a little late?" I ask.

"Yeah, no problem. I can't have my best artist all down in the dumps," he says loudly and I grin when Mischa pokes his head out of his room.

"I know you're just saying that to make Atlas feel better," he calls down the hallway, and Zeke and I grin at each other as he disappears back into his room.

I hear Nico chuckle in his room before the buzz of his tattoo gun starts back up.

"You really think she's 'the one,' Atty?" Zeke asks me and I look up at him, trying to see if he's making fun of me, but all I see on his face is genuine curiosity.

"I don't know but there's something about her that just clicks with me. I just... I just want to figure out why I can't get her out of my head."

"Well, you know what they say. The best way to get over someone is to get under someone else."

I shake my head at that. "That's the thing though, Z. I don't want anyone else."

He watches me for a minute, leaning against the front counter as he thinks it over.

"Shit, man. You got it bad."

I grin at him before I turn and log off the computer. My next client will be here soon and I need to go get everything ready. Zeke will take over up front until we close in a couple of hours.

He claps me on the shoulder as I pass and I try to

contain my glee. Zeke has been like the cool older brother that I never had and I value his opinion. Nico nods at me as I pass by his open door, giving me a small smile and I grin back at him. I have a feeling that if I asked him why he thought I couldn't get Darcy out of my head, that he could tell me. Deep down, I think I know too, but I don't really want to talk about it. Being ignored by my parents all my life has left me desperate for love and attention and part of me can see that Darcy is the same way. Before I head down the hall to my room, I check out the tattoo Nico is doing on a guy. I try to duck inside before Mischa can see me, but he's quicker. I already know that he'll be giving me a ton of shit over how happy an appointment is making me.

"So, she finally called," he says, grinning at me as he wiggles his eyebrows.

"Told you she would."

"Let me know if you want any tips. I can send you some more articles if you want? I'd hate to see you run your girl off again," he jokes and I flip him off.

I hear him chuckle as I head into my room and he gets back to his client. I don't need his tips but that won't stop him from sending me every dumb article or meme that he can find. He's right about one thing though. There's no way that I'm letting Darcy get away again. I pull out some fresh paper, drafting a few more possible designs for her before my client gets here. The teasing had been starting to die down the last couple of days but I know now that she's called, it's going to start all over again.

That should annoy me but deep down, I think that Darcy is going to be worth whatever teasing these guys can throw at me.

EIGHT

Darcy

IT'S FINALLY Tuesday and I've been nervous all day. Atlas and I have texted at least once a day over the last couple of days. It started out about the tattoo but we agreed on a design that first day and then we just started talking about other things. He's fun to talk to and I find that I'm more confident over text than I am in person. Seeing that he really is interested in me has been a huge confidence boost too. I don't have any experience with men but even I know that guys don't spend time texting girls that they aren't into.

He sent me some pictures of the design that he had drawn up already and I loved it. It was exactly what I had in mind and I was surprised that he had nailed it after only one brief conversation. The level of detail in it was extraordinary and I could see why he was booked so far in advance.

It was a minimalist design with a long thin stem and a few leaves branching off it. The stem would run up most of my spine and the line was so thin that you would have to look close to be able to see it. The three leaves will branch off to either side right below my shoulder blades. At the top is a flower in full bloom with a red watercolor design staining the petals.

It's beautiful and, when I showed Indie, she said it reminded her of me. The way the flower still blooms and is strong even with such a fragile looking stem. I'm glad that I didn't have to explain it to her. She knows me well and she knew why I wanted the design as soon as she saw it.

I towel off my hair, staring into my closet for something to wear tonight. I know that I'll have to take my shirt off and unsnap my bra but I still slip on my sexiest purple lace bra and matching panties. I pull on a pair of black leggings, the ones that Indie says shows off my ass before I pull a soft heather gray tunic over my head. I tie my hair up in another bun, wanting the wavy strands to be out of the way.

It's almost time for me to leave to head to the shop. I convinced Indie to go with me but I have a feeling that she's got a plan to sneak away and leave Atlas and me alone. She's been going on and on about "Plan Win Atlas" all week and step one of that plan was getting the two of us alone together.

I swipe on some mascara, taking one last look in the mirror before I head out to the living room to find her.

"You look hot!" she cries as soon as I step into the room.

"Thanks," I say, twirling in a circle for her.

"You're going to have him drooling," she says, giving me a low whistle as I turn to face her again.

She's dressed similarly to me in a black tank top with some funky patterned leggings on underneath. Her hair is pulled up into a high ponytail and she's still wearing makeup from work. She looks gorgeous and effortlessly cool and I do my best to stop comparing my body to hers.

"Are you ready to go?" I ask, trying to change the subject.

"Yeah, just need to grab my shoes."

We both slip our flip-flops on, locking the door behind us as we head out to her car. It's a nice night but too late to be walking around by ourselves, so Indie said she would drive us. It takes longer to drive than to walk with the late-night traffic but we still make it there before nine p.m.

Mischa is headed out the door as we walk up and he stops when he sees us. We smile and wave at him as we climb out of the car and head toward the front door.

"Hey, you two! Indie, nice to see you again. Darcy, Atlas has been dying to see you."

I blush at that and Indie elbows me in the side, an 'I told you so' look on her face. I roll my eyes at her.

"That's enough," Atlas says as he joins us, shooting a look at Mischa.

"Hey," I say shyly as he comes to stand next to me.

"Hey," he says with a sexy grin.

"Mischa! I am starving. You wanna grab a pretzel with me?" Indie asks, pointing over her shoulder to a street cart that looks like it's about to close up.

She gives him a pointed look, staring him down and he smiles at us before he agrees.

"Perfect. I was just about to grab a bite to eat."

He grins at Atlas, clapping him on the shoulder as he leads Indie away from the shop and over to the vendor. I sigh, glaring after her as she winks over her shoulder at me. I knew she was going to do that but I thought we'd at least make it inside the shop first.

"Ready to get started?" Atlas asks me as he holds the front door open for me.

He seems happy to be alone with me and I try to give myself a pep talk as I nod my head and walk ahead of him inside. *You can do this. He likes you. You know that, Indie says so, even Mischa says so.* He closes and locks the front door behind us and I glance at him as I wait for him to open the wrought-iron gate next. He takes my hand in his as we head back to his room.

I let him lead me inside and take in all of the artwork on his walls. I haven't seen his room yet and I take a minute to look around. It's clean, with everything in its place. The walls are the same pale blue as his eyes and unlike Mischa's room, where you could barely make out the paint color under all of the artwork tacked up, Atlas's room is more organized with everything neatly hanging on the walls and over his desk. Just like Mischa's though, the space is a little cramped and I have to edge my way around the table in the center of the room to drop my purse onto a chair in the opposite corner.

I look at some of the designs that he does have hanging up and I can see why he has such a long waiting list. He's talented, like really talented and I pull my hands from his so that I can walk around the room and look at all of the draw-ings hanging on his walls.

"You're really good," I murmur when I make my way around to his desk.

"Thanks," he says, sitting down in his chair and drag-ging over the paper with my tattoo design on it.

"It's even better in person," I breathe out as I take in the flower design.

"It's going to look even better on you. Are you ready to

get started? Or did you want a drink or to use the restroom or anything?"

I take a deep breath as nerves hit me.

"No, I'm good. We can get started."

"Perfect. I need you to take off your shirt and bra."

NINE

Atlas

SHE GAPES at me for a second and I realize that I probably should have eased into that a little more. I watch her take a deep breath before she rolls her shoulders back and lifts her chin. Her hands grip the hem of her shirt and she tugs it over her head. My mouth grows dry at the sight of her luscious curves almost spilling out of that purple lace bra. I clear my throat, trying to hide the bulge in my pants by spinning around in my chair and pretending to grab something off of my desk.

The tattoo table is already set up for her with the top part at an angle so that she can sit and lean forward. If she wraps her arms around the table, then she should be able to keep still while I tattoo.

"If you can sit on the table and wrap your arms around the top part, I'll get the tattoo outline lined up right. Then you can check it out in the mirror before we make it permanent."

"Okay," she says and I reach out, making sure that she makes it up onto the tattoo table okay. I watch as she gets situated before she reaches around and unsnaps her bra, slipping the straps down her arms.

I bite back a groan at the sight of her topless on my table. I picture turning her around and leaning her back on the table, face up. She could cup her tits and hold them for me while I took turns teasing the sweet peaks or maybe she would let me pull those tight leggings down and bury my face in her sweet pussy. *I wonder if she's wet.*

"Is this right?" she asks and I realize that she's been waiting on me for a couple of minutes while I stared at her and imagined doing dirty things to her.

"Yeah, that's perfect," I say, pulling out the rest of my equipment and moving to lay the outline on her back.

She's tan, like she spends a lot of time outside, with tiny freckles on the tops of her shoulders. She has a small scar underneath her ear on her left side and I want to lean in and brush my lips over the mark, but I restrain myself.

"How has your week been so far?" I ask as I clean off her back where the tattoo will be.

"Busy," she says with a sigh and I watch her shoulders slump a little bit.

"What do you do for a living?"

"I own my own business. Rose's Nursery and Land-scaping."

"No shit?" I ask, impressed.

"No shit," she says with a small laugh.

"I've heard of that place! Over on Michigan Avenue, right?"

"Yeah," she says, the surprise clear in her tone.

We're silent for a minute as I pick up the design and concentrate on getting it just right along her spine. I get it centered, double-checking that the leaves and petals are just right, with the flower part between her shoulder blades, about an inch down from her neck. Once I have the stencil on just right, I clear my throat and take a step back, looking at it from another angle to make sure that every line looks perfect. I take pride in all of my work, but I really want Darcy to love this, to be impressed by me.

I pull the paper away, leaving just the stencil on her back and I take a minute to admire the way it looks against her creamy skin. I love seeing her topless and I try my hardest to focus on the tattoo and not on Darcy's perfect curves. My hands itch to touch her and I shove them into my pants pockets.

"Ready to check it out before we make it permanent?"

"Yep," she says and I help her off of the table while she tries to keep her arms crossed over her large chest.

Her tits are plumped up under her arms and I wipe my mouth, making sure that I'm not drooling at the sight. I lead her to the back where there's a couple of mirrors hanging on the wall. They're situated in a circle so that Darcy can look in one mirror and see it in the others.

She keeps her arms tight across her chest, checking out her reflection in the mirror before she smiles at me brightly.

"It looks perfect! I love it!" she says, excited.

"Yeah, me too," I mumble to myself as I stare at her in the mirror.

She turns back to me and smiles and I can't help but return it. I lead her back to my room and help her back onto the table before I tug on my gloves and pick up my tattoo gun, trying to focus on her tattoo and not on what I'd like to be doing to her. My hands shake as I picture gripping her hips and driving into her from behind. I want to hear her say my name again. I want to make her scream my name and then make her say it on a breathy sigh.

I grip the tattoo gun tighter and let out a deep breath as I push those thoughts away and lean forward, pressing the needle to her skin.

TEN

Darcy

I JUMP as the buzz of the tattoo machine fills the air and Atlas places a hand in the center of my back, urging me to be still.

"I'm not going to lie; this is going to hurt. Most people get their first tattoos on their arms or somewhere that doesn't hurt quite so much. You seemed insistent that it be here though..." he says, his voice trailing off, and I know that he wants me to elaborate.

So much for him not knowing what I was like in high school...

I take a deep breath as Atlas goes back to my tattoo. I tense a little bit at first because, dang, it really does hurt, but as I start to tell him about myself a little, I find that I can focus less on the stinging sensation on my back.

"I had scoliosis when I was younger. Kids used to make fun of me because I had to wear a brace for a while. I had it taken off before my senior year but everyone still thought of me as that weird girl. That's why I wanted it along my spine."

"Dumbasses," Atlas mumbles under his breath but I still hear him and smile at the anger I hear in his voice. I have a feeling that Atlas would have been one of my few friends back then.

"I was chubby back then too and between my weight and the big metal brace, I was an easy target."

"You're not chubby. You're gorgeous. Those kids were idiots. I'm surprised that any of them even graduated high school. They should have been worshipping at your feet, not picking on you," Atlas states firmly and I can feel my cheeks heat at the power I hear in his words.

"Luckily, I had Indie," I say with a smile. "I wonder where she and Mischa are," I think out loud, realizing that we've been alone for a while.

"I'm sure they're still eating. Mischa won't let Indie go off by herself. He'll keep her safe."

I nod my head. I already got the impression that he was a good guy.

"So, you're from Pittsburgh then?" he asks as his needle moves higher up my back.

"Yeah, well, technically I was born in California but I don't remember it at all. My mom dropped me off here with my grandparents when I was three and I grew up with them."

He's silent as I take a deep breath, remembering the day she dropped me off and left, never to be seen by me again. I don't like thinking about her and I try to change the subject and lighten the mood.

"They lived kind of on the outskirts of the city, on this big piece of land."

I smile as I remember trips to the old nursery in town, picking out plants and flowers to bring home and plant.

"So, you've always liked flowers then?"

"Oh yeah," I say with a soft chuckle. "I was obsessed with flowers and gardening, even when I was really young. I used to do it with my grandma. We would plant flowers every spring and a garden too."

"So that's what the flower is for?" Atlas asks as he leans over to dip the needle into the little cup of ink and I sneak a look at his handsome face. His eyebrows are scrunched together like he's concentrating hard but I don't see any judgment on his face.

"Yeah. To remember them by and to remind myself that I'm stronger than I realize," I say quietly.

We're silent for a few minutes, the only sound the buzz of the tattoo gun and the music that he's playing from a tiny speaker in the corner of the room.

"When did they pass?"

"A couple of years ago. My grandpa had a stroke and my grandma followed a week after him. Died from a brain aneurysm, they said, but I swear it was from a broken heart. They were so perfect together. I've always wanted a love like that," I say wistfully and then clear my throat when I realize that maybe things are getting a little deep for our first real conversation together.

"What about you?" I ask, trying to change the subject.

"What about me?"

"What were you like in high school? What's your family like?"

His needle traces off of my spine and I figure he's up to the first leaf by now.

"I was pretty quiet in school. I liked to draw, so I spent most of my classes doodling in my notebooks."

"Did you always want to be a tattoo artist?"

"No. I mean, I knew that I wanted to draw or do art but it wasn't until I was sixteen that I got really into tattoos and the whole process. After graduation, I started to apprentice under an artist down in Philadelphia. That's where I'm from, by the way."

"When did you move to Pittsburgh?"

"A couple of years ago. I applied at a couple of shops after my apprenticeship and when I got hired at Eye Candy Ink, I moved up here."

"Is your family still down in Philadelphia?"

"Yeah. They still live in the same house that I grew up in."

There's something in his voice that lets me know that his family is a sensitive subject. I can understand that. I get sad every time I think about my grandparents passing or how my mother had just abandoned me on my grandparents' doorstep and never looked back.

We're silent for a little bit, just the buzz of the tattoo gun filling the silence and I try to focus on anything but the pain along my spine.

"Halfway done," he murmurs after a little bit and I nod. "Do you need a break or anything?"

"No, I'm okay."

"When did you open your nursery?"

"Right after graduation. I didn't really want to go to college, but my grandparents had left me some money and I used it to start the greenhouse and my first year's plants. The nursery opened the next year and I started the landscaping side the year after that."

I still can't believe that he's heard of me. I mean, I'm doing good, but I didn't think that people outside of plant and flower lovers would know about me.

"That's awesome. Zeke's friend was actually talking about looking for a new landscaper. I'll have to tell him to give you a call."

"Yeah, have him call me or he can fill out the form on my website and I can quote him on there too."

"I'll let him know."

"Thanks," I say as he moves between my shoulder blades.

"Hey, Darcy?"

"Hmm?"

"I think your grandparents would be really proud of you."

My heart flips over at his words. I didn't realize how badly I wanted to hear that until he said it. How does he know me so well already?

"I hope so," I whisper.

"I know so."

We slip into another stretch of quiet until the buzz from the tattoo gun stops.

"All done with the black. Now, we just have to do the red in the petals."

I turn my head, watching while he messes around with the equipment on top of his desk. I peek at the clock hanging on the wall and am surprised to see that forty minutes have already passed.

He'll be done with my tattoo soon and then it will be time for me to leave. *Will he ask me out? Should I ask him out?* My face flames at the thought of asking Atlas out and I try to hide it as he turns back around to me.

He moves behind me and I hear the tattoo gun click back on as I bite my bottom lip and try to figure out what I should do when the tattoo is done.

ELEVEN

Atlas

I FINISH the watercolor on the petals, careful to get it just right. I work hard on all of my tattoos but I want this one to be the best that I've ever done. I smile as I turn my gun off and turn to wet a paper towel, wiping off the excess ink until the tattoo is clean and visible. I lean back in my chair, admiring my work and taking a few more minutes to enjoy Darcy topless.

"All done. Are you ready to go check it out?"

"Oh yeah," she says, turning and grinning at me over her shoulder.

She crosses her arms over her chest again and I help her off the table and back to the mirrors. She turns around and I watch her face as she takes in the delicate tattoo running up her spine.

After I heard about her school days and how the kids had picked on her, I realized that her spine was the perfect spot for her tattoo. My hands clench into fists as I think about her being bullied and hurt by her classmates but I try to smooth out my features as she turns to face me.

"I love it! It's exactly what I had in mind," she says, spinning around to face me.

I watch in slow motion as her flip-flop gets caught on the other one and she starts to tip over. Her hands shoot out to brace her fall and I react before I can think, wrapping my hands around her hips and holding her against my chest. I keep my hands lower, wrapped around her waist, mindful of the fresh ink higher up her back.

Her hands are wrapped around my biceps, her bare breasts smashed up against my chest and I groan as my fingers reflexively grip her tighter. *I wonder if she can feel how hard I am right now.* Her pale cheeks are a bright red color so I'm guessing that, yes, she can.

I try to get my dick under control as I make sure that she's okay and steady on her feet. She shifts, her curvy body rubbing against me, and I moan as she rubs against my aching cock.

"I'm okay," she says as she looks up at me.

My eyes meet her bright hazel ones as I take in her dirty blonde hair tied up messily in a bun on top of her head, over her round cheeks and down to her mouthwatering lips. They're like a siren's call, drawing me in and I can't wait any longer. I need to feel her lips against mine or I swear to God I might die.

"You're perfect," I whisper against her lips, a second before I claim her mouth with mine.

Her eyes flutter closed as our lips meet but I look over her shoulder, watching in the mirror as she rises up on her tiptoes to get closer to me. Her arms wrap around my neck and I moan at the sight of my hands on her naked torso.

My eyes fall closed as I lick against the seam of her

mouth, desperate to get a taste of her. She opens for me, just as greedy for me as I am for her, and I push my tongue past her lips and rub it against hers in an erotic dance. She moans into my mouth, her fingers tangling in my hair and I grip her hips tighter. I'm sure I'm going to leave bruises and the thought of her walking around with my mark on her only gets me hotter.

Her kiss tastes like desire and longing. I've been thinking about this moment, about what she would taste like, what her lips would feel like against mine since the first second that I laid eyes on her and it definitely lives up to my imagination. Her lips are firm but warm and pliant as they move against mine.

I swipe my tongue against her lush bottom lip, giving it a quick, playful nip and she gasps, giving me the opening to slip my tongue into her mouth. I slip one hand up the back of her neck, cradling the back of her head and angling her mouth so that I can claim more of it with my lips. Her tongue tangles with mine and she moans into my mouth, deepening the kiss as we press closer together.

She tastes like heaven, like mint toothpaste and honey and I want to drown in the flavor. I never want this kiss, this moment, to end. I want to pick her up, to feel her legs wrapped around my waist. I want to rub against her there, between her thick thighs, until we both find our release. I'm about to try to make that fantasy a reality when I hear the front door slam closed and two people laugh as they enter the shop and start to make their way closer to us.

Damn Mischa and his rotten timing.

TWELVE

Darcy

ATLAS JERKS AWAY, stepping in front of me, and I blink out of my lustful fog to realize that Indie and Mischa are back. They're laughing up front and I blush as I realize that I'm standing topless back here with Atlas. I wrap one hand across my chest as Atlas turns and grabs my other hand, pulling me down the hallway behind him.

My lips still tingle from our kiss and I want to reach up and touch them but I'm worried that would give too much away. I wonder if Atlas can tell that was my first kiss back there. His thumb rubs against the back of my hand as he leads me into his room and closes the door behind us.

"I just need to dress and bandage it now so that it stays clean while it heals."

I nod as I turn around, giving him my back. He pulls gloves on and smears some kind of ointment over my spine, taping a bandage over the ink.

"All set," he says as he passes me my shirt. "You might

not want to wear your bra right now. Too much rubbing against it could irritate the tattoo."

I slip the shirt over my head, tucking my bra under my arm as I turn around to face him. My boobs are so big that it's obvious that I'm not wearing a bra. My nipples are still hard from our make-out session in the back and I look down to see them poking against the front of my shirt.

I look up to see Atlas staring down at them too with a hungry look in his eyes. He licks his lips and my thighs clench together as I picture his mouth on them, sucking them into his mouth and teasing me with his fingers.

He clears his throat as Indie and Mischa's voices get closer. My eyes dart to the door and I know that my window of opportunity is closing. If I want to ask him out, now is the time. Before we have an audience. I clear my throat, prepared to just blurt some dinner invitation out when Atlas beats me to it.

"Are you busy tomorrow?"

"What? Uh... no. Just work until six p.m."

"Good, I'll pick you up at six-thirty p.m."

"For what?"

"For our date?"

"Date?" I parrot back, beginning to feel like an idiot but this has never happened to me before and I feel off balance.

"Yeah, I'm taking you out to dinner."

I gape at Atlas, my cheeks heating as the door opens behind me.

"Hey, you two!" Indie says as she bounces into the room.

"Hey," Atlas says, his eyes staying locked on me.

"Are you all done, Darcy? Can I see it?" Indie asks, moving closer and trying to peek down the collar of my shirt.

"I'll show you at home," I tell her, shaking her off of me. She pouts but lets it go.

"You ready to go?" she asks me, looking between Atlas and me.

"Yeah, I just need to pay," I say, digging in my pocket for the cash I got out of the ATM this morning.

"It's on me," Atlas says, waving off my money.

"You don't have to do that," I try to tell him as I offer him the money again.

"I want to. Trust me, it's fine."

"Thanks," I say quietly.

"Anything for you, Darcy."

Indie looks back and forth between us with a knowing look on her face and I look down to the floor, trying to hide my blush from her.

"See you later, Atlas!" she calls as she turns to Mischa who is still standing in the doorway.

"Thanks for dinner," she says, smacking a loud kiss on his cheek and hugging him before she pushes past him out into the hallway.

Mischa looks thrown off, a shocked look on his face and my mouth drops when I see a blush stain his cheeks as well.

"Here are the aftercare instructions," Atlas says, handing me a piece of paper.

"Thanks," I say, folding it and shoving it in my pocket as I head for the door.

"See ya," I say, waving quickly to them both.

"I'll see you tomorrow, Darcy," Atlas says, a promise in his eyes.

I nod at him over my shoulder as Indie and I make our way out to her car and head toward home.

THIRTEEN

Atlas

I KNOW how busy Darcy and I both are from our texts over the last couple of days. She works early in the morning until five p.m. and then does office work until six p.m. I don't start at Eye Candy Ink until eleven a.m. and I work until nine p.m. Not exactly an ideal schedule for dating or getting to know someone. I have two days off a week and today is one of them.

I texted Darcy this morning to check on her tattoo and make sure that we were still on for tonight. I had to run some errands this morning and then I spent this afternoon googling restaurants and trying to find the perfect spot to take Darcy to.

I've never taken a girl out on a date before but I know that most girls want something more than fast food or pizza, especially on the first date. I made reservations for the two of us at some fancy brewery downtown. Abernathy Brewhouse. Mischa said the food was good and the pictures of the inside looked date-y.

Darcy had texted me her address earlier this afternoon and I head over there now. She doesn't live that far from Mischa's and my place actually, and it's only a couple of blocks from the tattoo shop. I park my car in a spot out front and hop out, trying to take a couple of calming breaths as I head up to her apartment.

I don't know why I'm so nervous. Sure, this is my first date as an adult but I've hung out with girls before and I was never this anxious. *It's because Darcy is special*, my subconscious whispers, and I know that it's right. I might not know Darcy that well yet but she means something to me already. I think she's the one.

I reach her floor and walk down until I find her apartment number. I wipe my sweaty hands on my dark jeans as I knock on her apartment door, waiting impatiently for the door to open. My jaw just about hits the floor when the door swings open and I get my first look at Darcy. *Yeah, she's the one for me*, I think, and my dick jerks to attention in my pants, agreeing.

"Hey," she whispers and I gulp, my wide eyes traveling from her toes peeking out of her wedge sandals, up her shapely calves and curvy hips, encased in a snug black dress that ends mid-thigh. Her waist nips in and then curves up to form the perfect hourglass shape and my mouth waters as I see the deep V-neck of her dress. It hugs her tits perfectly, plumping them up and my fingers flex as I imagine what they would feel like in my hands. Her dress is a halter style and the straps wrap around her neck. Her back must be bare and I wonder if her tattoo is showing.

She's wearing little makeup, just some mascara and lip

gloss. Not as much as I'm used to seeing on girls, especially the ones who come to the shop. It's good though. Darcy doesn't need all of that. She's beautiful just the way she is. Her hair is up again today and I get the feeling that she doesn't like wearing it down. I don't mind, it gives me easier access to her neck.

"Hey," I blurt out when I realize that I've just been staring at her for a solid minute.

She giggles and turns to say goodbye to Indie who I see is curled up on the couch, a laptop balanced on her knees.

"Have fun, you two!" she calls after us and I wave as Darcy closes the door.

I lead her down to my car, opening the door for her and helping her in before I round the hood and slip behind the wheel.

"You look beautiful," I tell her as I cup the back of her head and lower my lips to meet hers.

Her lips part under mine right away and I slip my tongue into her mouth. She sighs against my mouth, her fingers curling in the front of my black button-down shirt as she holds me against her. *Yeah, like I'm going to try to get away from her.*

A car horn blares next to us and we jerk apart, both of us panting. I shoot a glare over my shoulder at the other driver as I turn the ignition and shift into drive.

"Hungry?" I ask her.

"Starving," she says.

My dick hardens further and I shift, trying to find some relief in my jeans that have become too tight.

Down, boy.

FOURTEEN

Darcy

I TAKE in Atlas's dark wash jeans and his button-down shirt. He's got the sleeves rolled up to his elbows and a pair of scuffed boots on his feet. He looks casual but still hot as hell. His black hair is a little messy, like he's been running his hands through it.

He asks me about my day as we drive toward downtown and I try to focus on his questions instead of the lustful gleam in his pale blue eyes. We park in the lot for Abernathy Brewhouse, some new brewery that opened up a couple of months ago. I haven't eaten here before but I've heard good things. I smile at Atlas as he offers me his hand as we get out of the car.

He leads me toward the front entrance and I smile down at our joined hands. There's a little bit of a wait at the front desk and I lean against the wall next to him as we wait for our table to be cleared. Atlas leans down and brushes a loose strand of hair behind my ear, grinning down at me.

I look away from him and notice a few people giving us weird looks. At first, I think it's because of my curvier form or the fact that someone who looks like Atlas is with someone who looks like me but then I realize that most of the stares are at Atlas. I figure that the girls are checking him out until I see a girl wearing a cardigan buttoned all the way up scrunch her nose up at him.

It's the tattoos and piercings, I realize, and I glare back at her when she catches me watching her. She turns away and I turn my back on her, hoping that she catches a look at the new tattoo on my back. I wore this halter dress specifically to show off my new ink. Plus, I was worried about anything rubbing against it still.

The hostess calls our name and we follow her through the crowded restaurant to a high table in the back. Atlas helps me into the taller chair, his hands grabbing my hips, and he lifts me effortlessly onto the tall stool.

"Thanks," I murmur and he smiles at me, leaning down to whisper in my ear.

"Anything for you, Darcy."

I shiver as his warm breath fans over the shell of my ear and his hand grips the back of my neck, squeezing lightly as he takes his own seat next to me. His jean clad knee brushes against my bare one and I shift on my chair, wanting to feel more of him pressed up against me.

For the millionth time, my mind flashes back to our kiss last night in the back of the tattoo shop. I can't get the way he felt pressed up against me out of my mind. That hard bulge in his jeans pressing into me or the way his hands had held me still while his mouth moved over mine. When his tongue slipped into my mouth, it had almost felt like he was branding me.

I try to clear my dirty thoughts and reach across the table, sliding a menu over to look at.

"Have you been here before?" I ask and immediately images of him bringing all of his dates here pops into my head.

"No, but Mischa came here with Sam a couple of weeks ago and said it was really good."

My body relaxes knowing this isn't his usual date place and he reaches his hand out, sliding his fingers over the back of my hand.

"Are you okay?"

"Yeah. I'm good," I say, turning back to my menu.

We're quiet as we look over the choices and I decide on a burger and some sweet potato fries. I set my menu aside, looking around the place. It really is pretty with exposed brick walls and wood floors. There's a distressed mural on one wall with the brewery name painted in a graffiti style and the bar runs along the opposite wall.

I notice some other patrons looking our way and I turn slightly in my seat, trying to see if there's something behind me. I frown when I just see a plain brick wall and turn back to see them looking at Atlas. They give him a dirty look before they turn back to their meals and I frown at them.

"It's because of my tattoos," Atlas says and my eyes jerk to meet his.

"Does it bother you?" I ask, glaring at the couple who had been giving him the dirty looks.

I look back to him when I hear him chuckle and see him giving me an adoring look.

"Nah, I'm used to it now. Who cares what those random strangers think?" he says, pointing his thumb over his shoulder in their direction. "I like who I am."

I search his face but see that he's telling the truth.

"I do too," I say softly but I know he still hears me, even over all of the noise in this place.

The waitress comes over then and takes our order. Atlas orders a burger too but he gets his on a pretzel bun and with regular fries. Once she's gone, he picks my hand up in his, brushing his thumb over the back slowly as he asks me more about my greenhouse and landscaping business and what growing up here with my grandparents was like. I tell him about some of the crazier things that Indie and I did when we were younger and we laugh as we eat our food.

"I'll gave your number to Zeke. He's got a friend who owns a couple of restaurants and he was just talking about redoing the landscaping on the back patio of one. He should be calling you soon."

"Yeah, go ahead. I'm still trying to grow that side of the business, so that would be great. I've always been more into the growing side of it but landscaping can be a big business."

I smile at him as I drink the last of my beer and wipe my hands off on my napkin. We wait for the waitress to come by and I tell him more about my greenhouse and the plants that I grow there.

"Can I see them?" Atlas asks after I tell him about some of the new flowers I tried to grow this year.

"Right now?" I ask him as he pays the check.

"Yeah, I don't have anywhere else to be," he says as he offers me his hand and helps me down off the chair.

He holds my hand as we walk back to his car, pulling me into his side when a breeze kicks up and I shiver slightly. I try to give him directions to my greenhouse, but he surprises me when he says he knows right where it is. Traffic is a little heavy so it takes us close to twenty minutes to make it over to the greenhouse. He parks in front and I dig my keys out of my clutch so that I can unlock the front door. The glass panes are slightly foggy from the difference in temperature and I can feel my hair start to frizz as soon as we step inside.

"This way," I say, pointing down an aisle after I flip on some of the overhead lights.

We walk down row after row of plants and flowers and I stop every few feet to explain what they are. Atlas seems interested and soon I get lost in explaining when the best time to plant each one is and when to harvest the vegetable and fruit plants. Before I realize it, an hour has passed and I blush as I turn to Atlas.

"Sorry, I think I got a little carried away," I apologize.

"No, don't be sorry. It was interesting and I love seeing you like this. So confident and passionate. It's intoxicating."

His voice gets lower as he turns to cup my face and lowers his mouth down to mine. Just like every other time we've kissed, as soon as his lips touch mine, I get lost in him. He tastes like the food we just ate and something that is distinctly Atlas, and I moan as my fingers thread through his messy locks. I grip the silky strands, holding him to me as we kiss, fogging up the windowed greenhouse even more.

I try to contain my grin as he drives me home, walking me up to my door and giving me another kiss goodnight. I debated inviting him in but I'm not quite ready for that yet, so a steamy goodnight kiss will have to tide me over until next time.

I fall asleep that night with my lips tingling, my body buzzing, and images of Atlas floating through my mind.

FIFTEEN

Atlas

I FEEL like I'm floating on cloud nine as I grin and practically run down the rows of plants at the nursery. My heart starts to race as I get closer and closer to the back office, where I know my girl is busy working. I don't have long before I have to head to Eye Candy and I pick up my pace, jogging until I reach her office.

It's been two weeks since my first date with Darcy and I've been trying to stop by the nursery with breakfast for us to share at least twice a week ever since. I want to spend more time with her, but with our crazy work hours, we don't get to see each other as much as I'd like. We've been finding ways to make it work though. I bring her breakfast when I can and sometimes, we meet up for lunch or dinner when I'm between clients. We even went out to Captain's Bar after I got off one night and had some drinks. I know it's hard for her to stay up so late, since she has to get up early and it means a lot that she's making sacrifices to be with me.

I've taken her out on more dates my last two days off too. We went to see the newest romantic comedy playing on Wednesday and to an art gallery opening the week before that. She let me hold her hand throughout the movie, as we shared a bucket of popcorn and I felt giddy, like I was a teenager again as we sat in the dark, pretending to watch the film. The art gallery was interesting too. I loved hearing her opinions on each of the pieces and I was thrilled that we seemed to share an interest in art, or at least a similar taste in the art that we liked.

I have another five days before my next day off and it feels like the time is dragging. Normally, I love my job and designing new tattoos for my clients, but lately, all I've wanted to focus on is when I'll be able to see my girl again.

Mischa has been giving me worried looks all week. He keeps trying to warn me to slow down but I don't want to take things slow with Darcy. I've never met anyone like her, so strong and tough on the outside but sweet and soft on the inside.

I know that Mischa is just worried about me getting hurt, but it feels like Darcy feels the same way about me already as I do for her. Nonetheless, he still keeps telling me that I should play it cool and take my time with her.

Mischa knows a little about my parents. He had asked about them after I had lived with him for a couple of months and they never came to visit or called me. To be fair, I wasn't trying to call them either but he had noticed and I had admitted that we weren't close. I had told him a little about how busy they always were when I was younger, and I think he thinks that I've latched on to Darcy because I'm dying for love and attention. That might be true on some level but it's more than that.

If attention was all that I wanted, then I could have

hooked up with most of the girls who sat in my tattoo chair the last couple of years. That's never been my style though. If I'm being honest, I wasn't even looking for a girlfriend when I first saw Darcy. I was happy with how my life was, with my job and the family that I had found at Eye Candy Ink.

Seeing Darcy and talking to her that first day kind of knocked me on my ass and I haven't been able to figure out which way is up since. I'm not sure that I want to untangle myself from her. I like being trapped in her web.

I push open the office door and smile as she looks up from her computer and waves at me. She's on the phone and I take our breakfast out, setting it on her tiny desk before I cram myself into the chair across from her. Her office is cramped and there's barely enough room for the two of us but as long as I'm with her, I don't mind.

She drops her phone back down into the cradle and lets out a breath. I grin at her as I slide her coffee and breakfast sandwich over to her.

"That was Zeke's friend, Maxwell," she says as she takes a sip of her coffee.

"Did he hire you?"

"Not yet. I need to go see the properties and then I can draw up a landscaping proposal, and if he likes my ideas, he could hire me."

"I'm sure he will. Your ideas are the best!"

"You've never seen my landscaping projects," she says with a small chuckle.

"I don't have to. I'm sure you're the best."

"Thanks," she says with a blush before she bites into her breakfast sandwich.

We finish breakfast quickly and I kiss her goodbye so that she can get back to work.

SIXTEEN

Darcy

I WIGGLE around on the sectional, trying to burrow into the cushions more. It's Friday night and Indie and I are at home, lying on the couch, eating takeout Chinese while we catch up on episodes of Barry. It's been a long week at work for both of us and we decided that we just needed to relax and veg out tonight.

Indie tosses her empty takeout containers onto the coffee table, groaning as she collapses back onto her section of the couch.

"Ugh, I ate way too much," she complains, rubbing her flat stomach.

Envy floods me as I stare at her lithe frame. *Indie is so thin and pretty. She can eat anything and still remain the same tiny size. Why can't you be like that? Maybe you should try a new diet.*

The food that I just ate turns to a ball inside my stomach and I try my best to force those thoughts away. I wish that I could just be happy with my body the way it is. Why do I always have to put myself down or see the worst? 170 pounds isn't that bad. Sure, I can't fit into her size four jeans but Atlas seems to like me just the way I am.

I smile as I think about Atlas, blushing as memories from yesterday morning enter my mind. I can feel my cheeks turning pink and my lips start to tingle as I remember that kiss at breakfast. I had been ready to toss everything off my tiny desk and beg him to take me on it.

"You're thinking about Atlas, aren't you?" Indie asks, her tone smug as she smirks at me from her corner of the sectional.

"Of course not," I say, my face flaming with the lie.

Indie chuckles, dragging down the soft pink throw from the back of the couch and cuddling under it.

"Liar, but it's okay. I can always tell when you're thinking about him. You get this dreamy look on your face and these tiny hearts start popping up in your eyes. It's adorable."

I groan and toss one of my chopsticks at her. She manages to duck before it can smack her in the forehead and she smirks at me, sticking her tongue out at me as she mocks my aim with her eyes.

"I do not get some dreamy look on my face and my eyes have never had hearts in them."

"Whatever you say, Darcy."

Barry comes back on screen and we both quiet down, getting lost in the show but I know that she'll be back on me, asking me questions about Atlas and what's going on between us at the next commercial break. I stare mindlessly at the TV but I can't seem to get Atlas out of my head. He seems perfect, so sweet and charming, but I've found that most things that seem to be too good to be true, usually are.

Before I can think too hard about it, another commercial break comes up and Indie is twisting to look at me.

"So...?"

"What?" I ask, feigning ignorance.

She rolls her eyes at me, reaching under the blanket and tickling my foot.

"So, what's going on with you and Atlas. He's obviously into you, and you're into him. Are you guys like officially together now?"

"I don't know. He didn't like, come out and ask me to be his girlfriend or anything," I say, trailing off as doubts start to swirl in my head.

"I don't think people do that these days. No one is asking anyone to go steady with them anymore. You're like Instagram official and stuff."

"I'm not really into social media," I mumble.

"I know. Does he text you a lot? Has he asked you out again?"

"Yeah, we text all of the time. Like constantly almost and he asked me out after our date the other night but he only has two days off a week, so it's a little hard to find time to go out."

"Then I'd say that you're together. Aww, look at Darcy and her first boooyyyfriend!"

She practically screams boyfriend and I cringe, blushing as I pinch her pinky toe. She yelps and jerks away, glaring at me. I laugh at her as she pulls the blanket around her head, making a cocoon out of it as Barry comes back on. We're silent as we get lost in the show again.

"I'm glad you found him, Darcy. I know you don't trust people that easily, and I don't know how Atlas managed to get past your defenses so quickly, but I'm delighted for you. It's really nice to see you so happy."

I don't know how Atlas managed to get close to me so fast either but I know she's right. I look over to Indie and smile at her before I lean my head on her shoulder. She pulls the blanket away from around her head and wraps it around my shoulder, tucking us both under the soft material.

"Love ya, Indie."

"Love you more, Darcy."

SEVENTEEN

Atlas

I SNEAK a peek at my phone, smiling when I see what Darcy sent back. We've been texting nonstop for the last three days, sending each other texts when we wake up and before we fall asleep. She sends me pictures of some of her favorite plants in her greenhouse and today she sent me some pictures of the landscaping that she was working on.

My next day off isn't until Wednesday, three whole days away, and I'm already trying to come up with plans for our next date. Mischa will be at work and I was going to suggest dinner and a movie at my place but I'm not sure that I have the self-restraint not to throw her down on the first available surface and bury myself between her curvy thighs.

I'm all in with Darcy but I'm not sure that she's quite there yet and I don't want to try to move things too fast and push her away. She seems a little skittish, a little unsure, and I want to make sure that she's comfortable with me before we take the next step. I'm just not sure how exactly to do that.

Eye Candy Ink is closing and I clean off my workspace, getting everything ready for tomorrow morning before I head up front. Mischa had today off, so it's just Sam, Nico, and Zeke here with me. Zeke is in the back doing payroll and I don't want to disturb him, so I head up front to wait with Sam and Nico.

Nico is sitting in the waiting area, sketching, while Sam is behind the computer, scowling at the screen. The scheduling system still isn't fixed but Mischa asked Indie to come and take a look at it. Hopefully she can help because if it isn't fixed soon, I think Sam might snap and throw the whole computer against the wall, stomping on it until it's nothing but broken pieces.

She slams her hand down on the keyboard as I pass so I decide to leave her alone. I head into the waiting room and take the seat next to Nico, glancing over at the drawing pad resting on his knees. He's drawing a butterfly in a Japanese style. It's big, probably a chest or back piece.

"Looks badass, man," I tell him as I get comfortable in my chair.

He nods slightly and keeps drawing. We sit in silence for a minute, waiting for Zeke to be done with payroll and for Sam to be ready to head home.

"Have you ever been in love, Nico?" I ask and his pencil immediately stops.

It hovers over the page for a second before he rolls his shoulders and goes back to it.

"No," he says finally, never once looking up from the page.

My phone dings in my pocket and I glance down to see

a goodnight text from Darcy. I respond quickly, smiling as she sends back a sleeping emoji.

"Might want to avoid asking Mischa that question. He's already giving you enough shit."

I laugh at that and Nico smiles as he starts to shade in part of the butterfly.

"I can handle Mischa and his teasing."

Zeke walks down the hallway then and grins at that.

"Are you sure about that? He had today off. He's probably been thinking up new jokes all day."

We all laugh at that and Zeke comes over to sit down next to me as Sam runs to the back. It looks like she's already turned off the computer and I know that we'll all be leaving soon.

"Have you ever been in love, Zeke?" I ask him.

"Jesus, man! You're just giving Mischa more ammo."

I roll my eyes before I try again. I was hoping that someone could give me tips on how to win Darcy over but it looks like I've come to the wrong place.

"How do you make a girl fall in love with you?"

Nico sighs and Zeke shifts next to me.

"I wouldn't know. I've never tried before," Zeke says after a minute, a frown pulling at his lips.

We both turn and look to Nico who still hasn't looked up from his sketch pad but he must feel our eyes on him because he shrugs.

"I don't know. Just treat her right, I guess," he says, tucking his pencils and pad away in his backpack as Sam comes back up front.

"This about Darcy?" Zeke asks.

"Yeah."

"You're that far gone on her already?" he asks.

"Yeah, she's the one for me. I know it. I can feel it in my bones. I just need to get her to feel the same way about me."

We're silent as Sam grabs her bag and finishes up behind the desk.

"I wouldn't worry about it, man. From what Mischa has said, she likes you too. Girls go crazy for you; I'm sure Darcy is the same."

"That's just it though. She's different from those girls. From any girl that I've ever met." I murmur.

Zeke claps me on the shoulder and stands to help Sam lock up the iron gate and I watch him go.

"I wouldn't worry about it, Atlas. From what I saw the other day, she's just as into you as you are in her," Nico says as he moves to stand.

"Thanks, man," I say as I trail after them out the front door.

Zeke locks the door and I wave goodbye to him and Nico as I walk Sam to her car.

"You're not going to ask me?" she says as we head down the street to the parking lot on the corner.

"I was afraid you'd punch me if I asked you," I tease her and she smacks my arms.

I chuckle but turn to her.

"Have you ever been in love, Sam?"

"Hell no!" she says immediately.

"Then why did you want me to ask you?" I exclaim.

"Just seemed like if you wanted a female perspective that you would ask the only girl that you know."

"Okay then. How do I get Darcy to fall for me?"

"Treat her good. Find out what she likes and try to take an interest in it. Support her, try to do something every day to make her happy, and be honest with her."

"Is that it?" I ask when she's done listing things.

"Yeah, dumbass. That's it."

I wait while she climbs in the car before I turn to head to my own. She passes me as she drives out and flips me off and I grin and wave after her. She might be prickly on the outside, but deep down, Sam is a marshmallow. I can't wait to see her find a guy who can make it past her defenses.

I slip behind the wheel of my car and pause. I haven't seen Darcy in days and I miss her, so before I can overthink things, I pick up my phone and send her a text.

ATLAS: **U still up?**

I TAP my fingers against my thigh, impatiently waiting for her reply. Three little bubbles pop up and my heart starts to race.

DARCY: **Yeah. Can't fall asleep.**

Atlas: I'm on my way over. Maybe a good-night kiss will help

I START my car and grin as I drive over to her apartment. The lights in her apartment are off except for one. I send her a text, letting her know I'm outside, and she buzzes me in immediately. I take the stairs two at a time up to her floor.

She's waiting in the doorway for me, leaning against the doorframe wearing just a thin tank top and a pair of tiny sleep shorts. My hands grab for her as soon as she's within reach and my lips crash down onto hers.

Her hands grip my biceps, clinging to me as I devour her. Her hair is down for once and I reach up, tangling one hand in it as I cup the back of her head. I angle her head more as my tongue pushes past her lips and into her mouth, moaning at her minty taste.

"I missed you so much," I whisper against her mouth before my lips land on hers once again.

Her hands ball into fists in my shirt and she tugs me after her as she walks backward into the apartment. I follow her happily, backing her into a wall and pushing the front door shut with my boot behind us.

I pin her against the wall, using my hips to keep her in place while we make out. Her tongue flicks against mine and I groan. My hands trail up her sides until I can cup her tits. I've been dying to get my hands and mouth on them for weeks and they're even better than I imagined.

She moans and rests her head back against the wall as my fingers pinch and tease her nipples through her thin shirt. She gasps when I roll the stiff peaks between my fingers and I watch her face as I continue to play with the soft mounds.

I want to taste her. I want to peel off every single layer that separates us and lick and suck and bite every inch of her. As if she can read my mind, Darcy blinks her eyes open and bites her bottom lip.

"My bedroom is that way," she whispers, rolling her head in the direction of the hallway.

I stare down at her flushed face and lust-filled eyes.

"Are you sure?" I ask her.

"Oh yeah," she says, taking my hand and dragging me after her down the hall.

We enter her bedroom, and I glance around quickly as she closes the door behind us. There's a dresser on one wall, next to a door that I'm assuming is a closet. Her bed is unmade and I picture her lying in it before I got here, thinking about me. Her curtains are open slightly and I can just make out the hamper overflowing in the corner and the shoes lined up next to the door.

Darcy walks over to the bed, her fingers tangling in the hem of her shirt as she watches me. It looks like her nerves are back and I hate that she doesn't feel confident in her own skin. She's drop-dead gorgeous, the girl of my dreams. How can she not see that?

"We don't have to do anything, you know. I'll wait until you're ready."

"I am ready. I just... don't know what to do," she says quietly.

"I'll show you," I whisper as I step closer to her, kissing her slowly until she's lost in us again.

I knew that Darcy was inexperienced but I didn't realize just how much of a turn on I would find that. Knowing that I'll be her first, and if I have any say in it, her last, has my cock leaking in my jeans. I'd wait forever to be with her but now that she's here offering herself to me there's no way that I'm going to let the opportunity pass by.

I reach for her shirt and she raises her arms, helping me tug it over her head. Her arms come down quickly, covering her tits and stomach.

"I'm a little bigger than other girls," she says quietly and I grip her chin, forcing her to look up into my eyes.

"You're gorgeous. I love your curves. These," I say, reaching up and moving her arms away slowly so that I can cup her tits. I drag my hands down her sides and around to her ass, cupping the cheeks over the sleep shorts that she has on. "And this. All of you, every inch, drives me crazy."

She blushes but licks her lips, tipping her face up to me,

and I bend my head, meeting her lips halfway. My hands explore her curves as our tongues tangle and I slowly steer her back toward her bed. Her legs hit the mattress and I lower her down, hovering over her.

"I'm going to make this good for you," I promise her when she finally blinks her eyes open to meet mine.

My fingers go to her shorts and I pull them down her legs until she's laid bare before me. My cock leaks more precum into my jeans and I groan at the sight of her curvy body laid before me.

I come down over her, trailing kisses down her neck to her chest where I capture one stiff bud and suck it between my lips. I flick my tongue over her nipple, cupping the large globes in my hands and holding them together so that I can go from one to the other.

I lick and suck her tits until her nipples are red and swollen and wet from my mouth. Darcy is writhing beneath me, her hair fanned out on the mattress and her hands fisting the sheets.

"God, you're gorgeous," I whisper against her as I kiss over her stomach and between her legs.

I spread her thighs wide and kneel between her legs until I'm eye level with her pretty pussy. She's wet and dripping for me and I can't wait another second to find out what she tastes like.

I lean in and bury my face in her soft folds, getting lost in the scent and taste of her. I lick up her slit, my tongue finding her stiff nub and circling the sensitive button until Darcy's hands have stopped trying to cover herself. She grips the edge of the mattress and I smile as I suck her clit into my mouth and roll my tongue over it until she's crying out.

Her hips rock and I can tell she's close from the way her

breathing has changed to little breathy moans and gasps. I bring one hand up, spreading her pussy lips. My tongue trails down to her opening and I start to slowly thrust my tongue in and out of her snug hole while my thumb rubs tight circles over her clit. It doesn't take long and Darcy is screaming my name, her pussy pulsing on my tongue. I try to lick up all of her honey, not wanting to waste a drop.

I stand up, taking in her dazed expression and grin, loving that I did that to her. I pull my shirt off over my head and I watch her eyes heat as she takes me in. She hasn't seen me without my shirt on and I watch as her eyes take in my tattoos and piercings. Her eyes snag on my nipples, widening at the metal bars between each one. I'm hoping she's okay with them because there's one more that she hasn't seen yet and I would hate for it to scare her off.

My Prince Albert.

My hands rest on the button of my jeans and I debate if I should warn her or just take my clothes off and let her see. I decide to give her a little heads up as I unbutton my jeans and kick off my boots.

"There's something I haven't told you, Darcy."

Her eyes widen and she starts to sit up on the bed.

"Nothing bad! It's actually good. Really, really good," I say, my voice deepening as I think about the piercing rubbing inside of her and driving her crazy.

"I have more than just my nipples pierced."

I pull my jeans and boxers down and kick them off to the side. My hand strokes my stiff cock and I can tell the moment that Darcy spots the Prince Albert piercing. Her eyes widen and she lets out a gasp as she sits up all the way. Her eyes are glued to my cock and he loves the attention, growing even more and I keep up the steady rhythm.

"It will feel good," I promise her, and she looks up at me skeptically.

"Are you ready for me?" I ask, praying to every god that I can think of that she doesn't say no.

She nods, her cheeks a dark pink as she moves further back until she's in the center of the mattress. I climb on after her, kneeling between her spread thighs and lean over her, fitting my lips against hers as my cock brushes through her wet lips. She's still soaked from her last orgasm and I'm hoping that will be enough to stop this from hurting too much.

I keep kissing her as my cock slowly pushes through her folds and I start to sink into her tight warmth. She gasps against my mouth as I bury the first couple of inches inside of her and soon, I can feel her barrier against my tip. I tangle one hand in her hair while my other one comes up to play with her tits. I roll one nipple between my thumb and finger as I drive inside of her, popping her cherry and marking her as mine.

She tenses, her eyes squeezing shut and I take a moment to let her adjust before I start to rock into her slowly. I rest my forehead against hers, willing myself not to come already. Her pussy is gripping me so tight that I can already feel my balls drawing up and tingles starting at the base of my spine.

Darcy gasps and my eyes blink open, taking in her face as I thrust harder into her. My piercing drags over a certain spot inside her and I watch as her whole body lights up at the feeling. I angle my hips, making sure to hit that spot over and over again as I work between her legs.

She's close to coming again already and I lean up, bringing one hand between us so that I can play with her clit while I fuck her. Her eyes almost roll back in her head at the first touch of my thumb against her sensitive bundle of nerves and I grip her hips, pinning her to the bed.

She bucks against me and I grip her thighs, throwing her legs up onto my shoulders and wrapping one arm around her legs as the other goes back to playing with her clit. The new angle drives my cock into her harder, deeper, and Darcy braces her hands against her headboard as I pound into her, taking her roughly. Her back arches and she sucks in a deep breath. I reach up, covering her mouth with my hand right before she lets out a scream. Her pussy floods my cock and I can feel my own orgasm bearing down on me. She's so tight and hot that I can't stop the cum from shooting out of my cock, filling her womb as I follow her over the edge.

I pull out and collapse onto the bed next to her, wrapping my arms around her and spooning her from behind. She drifts off right away and I brush her hair away from her face, kissing her forehead and smiling as I close my eyes and follow her into my dreams.

EIGHTEEN

Darcy

I GOT HOME from work an hour ago and Indie was there working on her laptop. We talked about Atlas and last night already. She had come out and seen him kissing me goodbye this morning and she just about tackled me after he left. I told her about him texting me after he left work and wanting to come and give me a kiss goodnight, and then how it had progressed into sex. We giggled as I told her about how good my first time had been and she had sighed dreamily as I told her about waking up this morning with his head between my legs. *Now who is the one with hearts in their eyes*, I think with a secret smirk.

Indie went by Eye Candy Ink earlier today to take a look at their computer system. I tried to ask her about Mischa and Atlas, and she had given me a knowing smile. Luckily, she didn't toy with me or make me beg for the information.

"Atlas misses you."

"He did not say that," I say as my cheeks flame pink.

"He didn't need to. I swear he was glued to his phone. He kept grinning whenever you texted him. Oh my god, Darcy. It was so freaking cute. That boy is smitten. I swear to God, he's already in love with you," she practically gushes as she sets her laptop to the side and hangs over the back of the couch.

I try not to show how much her words have affected me but she's my best friend and knows me better than anyone, so I'm sure she can tell that I'm practically floating on a cloud of love.

She clears her throat and gives me a knowing look before she settles back on the couch and goes back to typing on her computer.

"Did you get the scheduling software fixed?"

"No, something was corrupt in the software so I had to erase all of it from their system and then I ended up putting some new software on for them that I developed last year. They should be all set now but I told them to call me if they had any more problems or issues with it."

"Did you see Mischa?" I ask.

Now it's her turn to blush and I grin at her as I watch her cheeks pinked. I knew that my suspicions about her liking him were spot on but so far, she hasn't said anything about him and I haven't pressed.

"Yeah, he was there," she says nonchalantly.

There's something in her voice though and I'm getting the impression that it didn't go well. I'm dying to know what happened, what he said, but Indie is the type to shut down if you push her on something. I decide not to pry right now, but I make a note to come back to the subject later. She never lets me deal with stuff all alone and I'm not going to let her have to face her problems by herself either.

"I've got some more work I have to get done tonight, so I don't think I'll be great company," she says as she types furiously on her computer keyboard. "Why don't you go see Atlas? You can surprise him at work and go out for some drinks or something after. I'm sure it would make his day," Indie says, pausing to look up from her computer screen at me. She wiggles her eyebrows suggestively at me and gives me a dirty smirk before she goes back to her work.

I glance at the clock, seeing that it's late, almost closing time. I could go down there and surprise him. Maybe we could go to a bar or club. Or maybe... an image of me showing up wearing only a trench coat flashes in my head and I bite back a grin. I really do want to go see him. I've missed him all day and I hate that we only get to see each other for a few hours each week. Texting and talking on the phone is good but it's not the same as seeing him face to face. My next date with him is in three days but do I really want to wait that long to see him again? He's always going out of his way to stop by the nursery and see me. Maybe now is my chance to return the favor. Show him that I'm just as into him as he is me.

"You going to be okay without me tonight?" I ask her as I head for my bedroom.

"Yeah, I'll be fine," she says with a smile. "Go get you some, girl!" she says, exaggerating the girl part.

With that decided, I spin on my heel and take off down the hallway for my bedroom. I hear Indie chuckle behind me and grin as I start to rummage through my closet. *What do you wear to surprise your boyfriend at work?* My mind snags on that word and I pause as I realize that this is the first time that I've called Atlas that, even if it was just in my head. Man, I've already got it bad and we've only been seeing each other for a couple of weeks. *Are things moving too fast?* Sure, we haven't done much physically, but my feelings sure seem to have gone from zero to a hundred fast.

I try to shake off the panic and doubts that come with those thoughts and think of something happier, like the two of us alone in the tattoo shop, kissing, or maybe doing a little more. I slip on a pair of wedge heels with some tight skinny jeans and an off the shoulder shirt. The clothes are a little tighter and more revealing than I would normally wear and I realize that my style has slowly been changing over the last two weeks.

Normally, I wear baggy, loose clothes in dark colors, stuff that swims on me, helps me blend in, and hides all of my curves and rolls. Ever since I started seeing Atlas though, I've been reaching for clothes that are actually in my size. Stuff that Indie bought me for my birthday or that I bought myself when I was trying to be more positive and confident in my own skin.

Something about Atlas just gives me that confidence that I've been searching for, fighting for, for most of my life. Sure, he's hot and walking around with him when he can't seem to keep his eyes or hands off of me is already an ego boost but I think it's more than that. I think I'm just inspired by him. He's so sure of himself and he doesn't let people's looks or whispers bother him. I wish I was more like that and it looks like he's already starting to wear off on me.

"I'll see you later. Don't work too hard," I call out to Indie as I make a beeline for the front door, excitement and nerves bubbling in my stomach with each step I take.

Indie blows me a kiss as I grab my keys and purse and head out the door.

"Don't worry! I won't wait up for you," she calls and I roll my eyes at her, closing the door behind me.

I climb into my car and thank god that the drive to Eye

Candy Ink is so short. I'm not used to driving in heels, or wedges, and I almost kick them off but luckily, I make it there safe and sound. A few feet down from the entrance, I find an open parking spot. I'm just wondering if the front door is already locked as I walk up and see Sam, the girl who is always behind the front counter, walking out. I speed up, hoping to catch her before she can close and lock the front door and I stop to say hi to her.

"Hiya, Darcy," she says as she holds the door open for me.

"Hey, Sam. Are you headed home?" I ask as I come to a stop on the sidewalk.

"Yeah, Atlas is with a customer still but she already paid, so there's no point in me sticking around. He's in his room though so go ahead and head back. I'm sure he'll be thrilled that you're here," she says with an eye roll and I smile at her, thanking her as I slip through the door.

We wave goodbye as she heads down the street and I take a second to admire the shop without all of the noise and people bustling around. It's quiet except for a faint buzz coming from the back of the shop. I know that it's Atlas's tattoo gun and I take a deep breath, squaring my shoulders as I quietly open the gate separating the front lobby from the tattoo artists' rooms and start to make my way back to Atlas's room.

My footsteps slow as I get closer to his room and I debate what to do now. Maybe I should have just waited in the lobby until he was done. He's with a customer and I don't want to just burst in but the door is open a crack and I peek in to see how far along he is. He's got to be close to done since it's so close to closing time. I peek around the doorframe, through the crack and my hand covers my mouth as I try to hide my gasp at the sight before me.

Atlas is standing next to the table, a half-naked girl gazing up at him adoringly. The girl is practically pressed up against him in nothing but a black, see-through lace bra and a pair of tight black leggings that show off her toned, perfect body. She's wearing a pair of heels that I would probably kill myself in if I tried to walk in them. I feel paralyzed as I stand at the door and watch as the girl leans into him more, her nails tracing teasingly over his bicep as she leans up on her toes, offering her mouth to him.

A stabbing pain takes up in my chest and I realize that it's my heart crumbling. I jerk away then and suddenly, all that I can think about is what Indie had said about the rumors of this place. That girls come here for more than just the tattoos and I choke back tears as I hastily back away from the door. I turn blindly and rush as fast as I can back to the front.

God, I'm such an idiot. He probably does this every week. Asks out a girl that he tattoos and then takes her out to dinner and sleeps with her. Sure, he didn't sleep with me but maybe I just wasn't as easy as he thought I would be. I can't believe that I thought I was special when I'm probably just one of many.

I slam the gate closed in my haste to get out of there, but I can't stop to care. I don't care if he knew that I was here. Let him know that I'm onto him and I'm not playing his sick game anymore.

I blink back more tears, my throat burning as I rush out to my car, peeling out of my spot and heading home as my heart breaks more in my chest. I rub my hand over the spot, taking a shuddering breath in as the tears start to fall on my cheeks. I can't believe that it hurts this much. *You were falling for him,* my mind whispers and I try to shut it off as I battle the light traffic back to my apartment.

I am almost sobbing as I park in my spot and I try to calm down a little before I head inside. I don't want to freak Indie out by coming home looking like this, although I'm sure that she'll be able to tell that there's something wrong. My phone dings with a new notification as I reach for the door handle and I look down to see a text message from Atlas. I swipe my finger across the screen, deleting it without reading his worthless words before I kick my car door shut and head into the apartment building, climbing the stairs up to our floor.

I try to close the front door quietly but when I turn around, I see Indie is still on the couch where I left here. She turns around to look at me, a smile on her face that instantly drops when she sees me. She takes one look at my tear-stained face before she hops off the couch and rushes over to me, wrapping her arms around me and helping me over to the couch.

"I've got you. It will be okay, Darcy," she says, just like every other time I've cried on her shoulder.

For some reason though, this time I don't believe her.

NINETEEN

Atlas

I HAVEN'T BEEN able to get hold of Darcy since yesterday afternoon and I'm starting to lose my mind. Hundreds of scenarios have flashed through my head, all of them terrible. What if she's been hurt, or in an accident? I'm at the shop tonight but my mind isn't on the work. All I can think about is my girl.

The other guys all seem to notice my mood and they keep shooting me worried looks. Even Mischa has been unusually quiet. It's almost closing time and I sit in the waiting room, clutching my phone and begging Darcy to text me back. I've tried to call her a couple of times today but it keeps going straight to voice mail.

"Alright, man. What's up with you today?" Mischa asks as he collapses into the chair next to me.

"It's Darcy. She hasn't been responding to my texts. I haven't heard from her since last night."

"Maybe she's just busy," he offers but I shake my head no.

"She always texts back. We text each other good morning and goodnight and she hasn't done either."

Mischa makes a gagging sound and I elbow him while Sam laughs from behind the counter.

"You two and your love make me sick," he jokes and I roll my eyes, a slight smile pulling at the corners of my lips.

Then I catch sight of my phone and the smile fades, worry replacing it.

"She seemed fine last night," Sam says and my eyes snap to hers.

"What? What are you talking about? You saw her last night? Where?"

"Here, man! She was pulling up when I was leaving and I held the door open for her. I thought you knew she was coming to see you. You were walking around staring at your phone with this dopey drugged up look on your face all day. I just assumed that you guys had plans."

I gape at her, my mind racing as I try to think back to everything that happened last night. The silence stretches in the room and Sam and Mischa exchange worried looks.

"She didn't come and see you? I thought you knew she was coming," Sam says again, shooting a cautious look at me.

"No, I didn't see her last night," I murmur.

The room is quiet and tense as I try to figure out what could have happened. I had a client and was the last to leave last night, but nothing happened. I remember the bang of the gate that I had heard as I was bandaging up my last client but I had thought that was just Sam leaving.

"Hey, why don't you head out. I can walk Sam to her

car and help her lock up and Nico is still with a client. Go get your girl," Mischa says and Sam nods.

"Thanks, guys," I say as I turn and bolt for the door.

I don't know what could have happened but I need to get to the bottom of it before I lose my mind. I try to think about where she could be as I get to my car. It's pretty late, so I figure that she's done at the greenhouse and is probably home. I head in that direction, cursing the heavy Saturday night traffic as I make my way slowly toward my girl.

I know if I can just see her, if I can just talk to her, that everything will be okay. Then we can get back to normal, back on track to our happily ever after. I already have our date for Monday planned.

I find a spot and park a block down from her apartment, getting out quickly and hurrying up the street. I manage to catch the apartment building door as someone else is leaving, and I take the stairs two at a time up to Darcy's floor. I knock on her door, waiting impatiently for someone to come and answer it. After what feels like an eternity, the doorknob turns and I step closer to the door, bracing my hands on the frame, anxious to get my eyes on Darcy.

Indie pokes her head through the crack and gives me a pissed off look. I'm not used to seeing anything but a smile on her face and my gut clenches. What the hell could have happened?

"Indie, is Darcy here? I haven't been able to get a hold of her all day," I say as I take a step toward the door of the apartment, trying to inch my way past her.

She blocks my path, shooting me another dark look as she tries to close the door in my face.

"Yeah, but she doesn't want to see you. You need to leave, Atlas."

"What? Why? What did I do?" I'm practically begging for answers now.

She gives a small shrug and my fingers tighten into fists. I want to push past her and go to my girl but I know that isn't the way to play this here.

"Please, just let me in. I *need* to see her. I need her."

She seems to waver for a second and I hold my breath as she bites her lip and looks over her shoulder, back into the apartment where I know my girl is hiding.

"Give me a second," Indie says as she closes the door in my face.

I run my hands through my hair, desperation coursing through me as I wait for Darcy to come to the door. After what feels like an eternity, the door opens again and I get my first look at her.

Her hair is in a messy bun on top of her head, some loose strands falling down around her face and neck. Her cheeks are red and blotchy, like she's been crying, and my heart breaks at the sight. I don't know what happened but I swear I will do anything to make it right.

"What's wrong, Darcy? I haven't heard from you all day. I was terrified something had happened to you," I say as I step forward and try to pull her into my arms.

She stiffens, pulling away and it feels like she just stabbed me in the heart.

"I saw you," she says and I stare at her, confused.

"Saw me where?"

"At the shop. With that girl last night."

"What girl?" I ask, more confused than ever.

"The half-naked girl that you were kissing last night. Listen, I get it, okay? You're a good-looking guy and I'm sure that you can have a different girl every night but I don't want that. I don't want to be one of the many. I'm not that type of girl."

I gawk at her, my eyes starting to burn with unshed tears. How could she think that I would cheat on her? I'm not that kind of guy. I don't see other girls. I don't see anyone but her and I thought that she felt the same way about me.

"What? No, Darcy, I don't want you to be one of many either. That—last night—that girl came onto me and I turned her down. I told her I had a girlfriend. I didn't kiss her, I swear! I don't even remember the girl. I don't want her. I don't want anyone but you," I plead with her, reaching out to take her hands in mine.

"I saw you with her and she was... perfect. Maybe you should be with someone like that," she says as she pulls her hands away from mine.

My throat feels itchy and I blink my eyes rapidly as she breaks my heart. I don't even think that she knew that she had been holding it in her hands all this time.

"I don't want her. I don't want anyone but you. You own me, Darcy. You have since the second that I laid eyes on you," I plead with her. She can't do this to us.

"You'll get over me," she says, starting to close the door in my face as more tears well up in her eyes.

I slam my hand against the door before she can close it all of the way and lean in.

"I'm never going to get over you. You're it for me. I know that you can feel that too or you wouldn't be this upset. You just have to trust me. Tattooing is my job, but I promise you that it's just that. Other girls don't mean anything to me. I don't see any of them. Only you. I only see you. Just give me a chance. Give *US* a chance and I swear that I'll prove it to you. I would never hurt you," I plead with her, begging with my eyes to not do this but she just shakes her head.

"I can't. I'm sorry," she says quietly as she closes the door in my face.

I hear the lock click into place as my head falls forward and bangs against the door and I gasp. I swear it feels like my heart was just ripped out and I'm starting to understand why no one at the shop has ever been interested in love. It fucking hurts.

After a few minutes, I straighten and push away from the door, heading back to my car. She just needs time. She'll come around and see how good we are together in a day or two and we can go back to being us.

Now that I found her, I'm not going to be able to let Darcy go. I know that I can make her happy, that I can make her fall in love with me. We just need to get past whatever the hell this is and then we'll be okay.

We have to be.

TWENTY

Darcy

I'M MISERABLE.

I've been a shell of a person walking around ever since I last saw Atlas and it's starting to wear on me. Every minute that I'm not at work has been spent curled up on our couch, watching movies and old reruns on TV. I've barely been able to concentrate on anything and I've had to stay late at work to keep up with the books. I'm just about to lock up and head home when there's a loud knock on the front door of the nursery. I frown, walking closer so that I can see who it is and my stomach sinks when my eyes finally adjust to the low light and I see Mischa standing there.

He gives me a small smile and a wave as he waits for me to open the door. I'm not sure that I can handle hearing whatever he has to say, but what choice do I have? I take a deep breath as I unlock the door and step outside.

"Hey, Mischa. What are you doing here?" I ask as I shut and lock the front door behind me.

"We need to talk. About Atlas."

My stomach sinks at his words and I squeeze my eyes shut tight, trying to keep myself under control as I turn around to face him.

"What about Atlas?"

"He's miserable, Darcy."

I close my eyes, trying to block out his words as my heart clenches painfully in my chest.

"I know that you haven't known him that long, but you have to know him better than this. He would never cheat on you. He's the best guy, the most loyal guy, that I've ever met."

"I saw him with—"

"You saw some girl hit on him. It happens to him all of the time. Girls throw themselves at everyone in the shop pretty much daily, but we never take them up on it. Atlas has never been like that. He's not the one-night stand type of guy. Dude, I'm not even a hundred percent sure that Atlas has ever even had sex!"

My mouth drops open at that and I gape at him as I try to process his words.

"Listen, Atlas might look like a tough guy but he's actually pretty soft. He... he's never really had a lot of people who care about him. His parents work constantly. He never really talks about them but I know that they were never there for him when he was growing up and they still barely talk."

I swallow, processing this new information about his parents and childhood. My heart breaks even more as I picture a young Atlas, all alone, waiting for his parents to show up to school talent shows or to pay attention to the new things he was drawing.

"He told me he only had one girlfriend in high school

and from what he said, it sounds like he was only with her to make his parents happy. She cheated on him and they broke up and he didn't even seem to care."

His eyes bore into mine, like this new information should mean something to me but I'm honestly still trying to catch up with everything that he just dumped on me. He sighs, his fingers tightening before he blows out a breath and continues.

"Do you even get what that means? He was with that girl for over a year and he didn't care when they broke up. He was with you for a couple of weeks and he's fucking devastated. All Atlas wants is to be loved. He's honestly a little desperate for it and I thought maybe he was rushing things with you, but... he dated that girl for a year and.... What do I know? Maybe love really can happen that fast. Maybe you really do see someone and just know."

"I-I..."

"Just listen to me right now, okay? Atlas is starved for attention, for someone to love. He hates being on his own. I mean, we both make enough that we could have our own places but he still chooses to live with me. And I don't mean that he just chose you randomly and that's why he likes you. I mean that he finally found someone that clicked with him. There's something about you that just fits with him. I thought you were going to be good for him, but you just ended up breaking his heart." His eyes narrow on me after he says that and shame washes over me.

"Atlas might come on a little strong, but he means well. I just wish that you would have let him explain. I wish that you would give him a chance."

He spins around to leave after that, takes one step, before he comes back to my side. I expect him to say something else, maybe yell at me, and I'm caught off guard when he points to my car, parked off to the side.

"I might be upset with you for hurting him but Atlas would kill me if I didn't make sure that you made it to your car okay."

I almost have whiplash from this conversation and I lead us over to my car in stunned silence. Mischa stands and waits patiently as I unlock my door and climb behind the wheel. He stands there as I start the car and shift into drive, nodding as I pull out before he heads over to his car.

My mind races as I think over everything that he just said. Maybe I should have given Atlas another chance. Maybe I should have trusted him when he said that nothing had happened. Was it really just all of my self-doubts that ruined this relationship? My stomach sinks as I realize that I might have brought all of this pain on myself.

I pull into my parking spot outside our apartment building and shut the car off. My phone dings and I close my eyes, already knowing who it is. Atlas has still been texting me every day even though I haven't responded or seen him in the last twelve days. I pick up my phone, my thumb brushing over the screen as I debate on what to do. *Maybe I should go talk to Indie. She'll know what to do.*

Indie has tried to talk to me every day but I just haven't been ready. She's brought home ice cream and pizza the first couple of days, but for the last week or so she's pushing for me to move past the wallowing stage and get back out there. She's been asking me to go out with her for the last couple of days and let off some steam, but I just haven't felt up to it. As my phone dings again though, I decide that maybe a distraction is just what I need.

I head inside and up to our place, finding Indie curled up on the couch with her laptop. She finishes typing and closes her laptop as I shut the front door behind me. She gives me a timid smile as she glances over at me and I can see how worried about me she is.

"Bar?" I croak and I watch a spark of relief flare to life in her eyes.

"Definitely! I can be ready in twenty," she says, tossing her laptop aside and darting down the hallway to her room.

I drag myself over to the couch and grab her laptop, plugging it in on the desk for her before I follow after her. I shower quickly, just rinsing off before I change my clothes and finish getting ready to go. I pull on some black jeans and a dark purple V-neck T-shirt, shoving my feet into a pair of Converse and running a comb through my hair. We're just going to the bar on the corner and I know that there will be some girls there dressed up more than me, but truthfully, I'm not in the mood to get dressed up or to be hit on. I need to process everything that Mischa said and think through all of this stuff with Atlas.

I shove my phone, ID, and some cash in my pockets before I go back to the living room to wait for Indie. I hear the water in the bathroom turn off and know it won't be long before she is ready to go.

Ten minutes later, we're in her car, headed to Captain's Bar, the dive bar down the street. Indie blares some pop music as we make the short drive and I smile slightly as she sings along, off-key with every word. She finds a parking spot and reaches out to stop me before I can get out.

"I'm glad you came out with me. I know the last couple of days have been rough, so let's go in there and relax. Try to have some fun, yeah?"

I take a deep breath and let it out slowly, releasing some of the tension that I've been carrying around for the last week. The first real smile that I've had in ten days stretches across my face.

"Yeah," I say, leaning over the center console and hugging her quickly before we both climb out and head inside the bar.

It's crowded since it's Thirsty Thursday and we push through the crowd until we get to the bar. Indie waves down the bartender and orders us each a cocktail as I look around the place.

I spot him almost instantly, his dark head bent as he sits at a table off to the side by himself. My heart breaks a little more at the sight of him and I'm turning to leave before I even realize what I'm doing. Indie grabs my elbow and keeps me next to her, following my eyes until she spots Atlas. We watch together as Mischa walks over and sets a beer down in front of him as he takes the chair across from him.

Atlas barely looks up but I catch a glimpse and can see the dark circles under his eyes.

"He looks miserable," Indie says as we continue to stare across the bar.

I nod, my eyes taking in every line of his body. The bartender places our drinks down in front of us, giving Indie a flirty look but she just slides a twenty across to him. I thank her, picking up my drink and taking a big gulp as I continue to watch Atlas and Mischa at their table.

"Maybe you should talk to him," Indie says as she grabs her own drink.

My eyes cut over to her and she holds her hand up to stop me from interrupting her.

"Just hear me out. You've been miserable ever since you two broke up and look at him. He's clearly in hell. I know that he's still texting you and trying to talk to you and you have to know that he really does like you. I know that you were upset about seeing him and that girl but, Darcy, he was just doing his job. Guys don't keep texting and calling if they aren't seriously into the girl."

I think about what she said and realize that she's right. Everything that she and Mischa said to me swirls in my head and I realize that they're right. If this wasn't real for Atlas then he would have moved on by now. He would be over there with a girl under each arm but instead he's staring dejectedly at his phone.

As if my thoughts have conjured them, two girls sidle over to their table and they try to sit down in the other chairs at the table. I watch as Mischa shoots a nervous look toward Atlas. He hasn't even looked up from his phone and I'm not sure that he realizes that there are other people at their table.

One girl reaches out to touch him and he jerks back at the contact, shooting the girl a dirty look as he sits back further in his chair. I watch his lips, trying to catch what he says to her but it's too dark in here to make it out. Whatever he says has the girls taking off quickly and I smile as they head to another table.

Indie and I finish our drinks slowly as we continue to watch their table. Three other girls try to come up and get close to him, and he turns them away quickly each time. My heart lifts with each girl that he shoots down and after the last one, I'm outright smiling.

Indie turns to me, taking in my face and smiling herself.

"If he didn't want you, then he could have taken any of those girls up on their offer. He doesn't know you're here, so it's not like he's turning down sex for your benefit."

I look back to him, watching as he starts typing on his

phone. My cell buzzes in my pocket and I take it out to see another message from him.

"He's out and he's still texting you, Darcy. That guy freaking loves you and I know that you really like him too. You let your mom leaving you mess with your head, but it wasn't your fault. She left because she was weak, not because of anything that you did. She should have chosen you, she should have been a better parent, but the drugs clouded her vision. You let those kids in high school put things in your head but they're not true. They weren't back then and they aren't true now. You've always been gorgeous and I think that you were finally starting to see that with Atlas. You were happier, more confident with him. He's good for you and you're good for him. You need to start seeing yourself more clearly and you need to trust Atlas."

I watch him for a minute and Indie leans in and gives me a hug.

"Trust *ME*, Darcy. That guy is never going to do anything to hurt you. Give him a chance."

I hug her back tightly.

"Mischa came to see me after work tonight.," I whisper against her shoulder and I feel her body tense.

Man, I really need to figure out what is going on between those two.

"What did he want? Was he bothering you? Is that why you wanted to come out tonight?" she asks, pulling back to study my face.

I shake my head at her, my eyes trailing back to Atlas.

"He just wanted me to give Atlas another chance."

We're silent for a moment and then I take a deep breath, squaring my shoulders.

"Will you come with me?" I ask her as she threads her fingers through mine.

"Of course," she says with a smile and I follow after her as she leads me through the crowd.

My heart starts to race with each step closer to their table and I smile as we finally come to a stop in front of them. Atlas looks up with an annoyed look on his face, probably expecting another pair of girls, and his eyes widen when he sees Indie and I standing there instead.

He looks even worse up close with bags under his tired eyes and several days' worth of scruff on his face. His hair is hanging limp around his face and he looks like he lost weight since I last saw him but as he takes me in his eyes start to brighten and a smile curves his lips.

"Darcy," he says as he jumps to his feet.

"Hi, Atlas. Hey, Mischa," I say, waving at both of them.

"Hey, Darcy, Indie," Mischa says with a relieved smile as he stands to greet both of us too.

Atlas hasn't looked away from me once, and I smile slightly as he hovers over me.

"Hi," I say again when he still doesn't say anything.

"Hi, hey," he sputters and I grin at how nervous he seems.

"Hey!" Indie says, taking a seat at the table next to Mischa.

"Can I get you a drink?" Atlas asks, seeming desperate to get me to stay.

"No... I was wondering if we could go somewhere and talk?"

His eyes jerk to me and he gulps.

"Yeah, yeah, of course."

He looks over to Mischa who rests his hand on the back of Indie's chair.

"I'll get a ride home from Indie," he says, nodding at us.

Indie smiles, giving me a thumbs up and I wave goodbye

at both of them as I follow Atlas outside to the parking lot. He holds the car door open for me and slips behind the wheel.

"Where did you want to go?" he asks as he starts the car.

"Back to my place?"

He nods, pulling out into traffic and heading back to my apartment building. He helps me out of the car, following after me as I head inside and up to my place. I unlock the door and lead Atlas over to the couch, turning the lights on as I go.

We sit facing each other and I smile as he shifts nervously next to me.

"I've been texting you," he blurts out and then he blinks like he's not sure why he just said that.

I giggle, loving that I can turn this big, strong, badass guy into a nervous mess.

"I know. Sorry that I didn't respond," I start. "I just needed some time. Seeing you with that girl—"

"I didn't do anything with her. I'd never do that to you," he interrupts, his face drawn tight with anxiety as he waits to see if I believe him.

"I know. I know that now. It wasn't you. It was me. I walked in and saw you two and you just looked right together. You fit. I've been made fun of most of my life. People picked on me about my back brace, about my mom abandoning me, about my weight and us together just didn't make sense to me. You're so perfect, Atlas, and it made more sense to me for you to end up with someone like her but I know that was just my own self doubts talking."

"Darcy, you're gorgeous," he says, a fierce frown marring his features.

"Thanks, and I know that I need to work on seeing myself in a more positive light. I know that and I'm trying, I promise. You were right. I like you and I want to try with you. If you still want me, that is."

"Oh, thank fuck," Atlas says, his palms cupping my face a second before his lips land on mine. "I want you, Darcy. I'll always want you," he whispers against my lips before his mouth claims mine once more.

I moan against his mouth, loving the feeling of his lips on mine, and I realize that I've missed this more than I thought. His tongue slips into my mouth and tangles with mine and I wrap my fingers in his hair, holding him to me as we make out like teenagers.

I don't know how much time passes before we hear voices out in the hallway. I pull away from Atlas reluctantly and grab his hand, pulling him off the couch and after me down the hallway into my room. I close the door behind us as Indie and Mischa come into the apartment. I can hear their voices in the living room and then the tv clicks on.

Atlas watches me in the dim light and I smile at him.

"Want to stay the night?"

He grins at me, wrapping his arms around my waist and tackling me onto the bed.

TWENTY-ONE

Atlas

I OPEN the door to the shop, making a quick stop at my room to grab the tattoo that I drew up last night before I head into Mischa's room. I grin when I see him yawning as he leans back in his chair.

"Morning," I say as I strip off my shirt and climb up onto his table.

He grumbles out a hello as he starts to pull out all of his equipment. I've been asking him to tattoo me for weeks and he finally caved and said he would do it this morning. Now, we're both here super early so that we can be done before the shop opens.

"Alright, what do you want done?" he asks, holding his hand out for the paper.

I hand it over to him, already anticipating him giving me shit.

"Fuck. Are you sure about this, man?"

"Absolutely," I say right away.

"Are you being blackmailed?" he asks, his face completely serious.

"MISCHA!" I shout, rolling my eyes at him. "No, I'm not being blackmailed. I love her."

He can barely hold back his look of disgust at the word.

"There are other ways to show her that you love her," he argues.

"Yeah, and I'm going to marry her just as soon as I know that she's ready."

For a second, I think Mischa is going to have a heart attack at the mention of marriage. He studies me, but when he sees that I'm serious, he turns around and grumbles under his breath about suckers as he starts pulling out everything that he'll need.

"Just black or did you want some color?"

"Black outline with a blood-red inside."

He nods, pulling down the ink and fitting a new needle onto his gun. He tosses me some antiseptic and some cotton balls and I clean off the area over my heart as he pours some ink into the caps and pulls on his gloves. He frowns as he lays the outline against my pec, making sure that Darcy is centered directly over my heart, and I know that this is basically torture for him. Mischa has refused to tattoo clients who wanted their girlfriend's or boyfriend's name on them, saying that he didn't want people to regret his work when things inevitably went south between the two. Him doing this just proves to me what a good friend he is.

Mischa steps back, double-checking the outline to make sure it's in the perfect spot. He nods before he looks up, eyeing me one last time.

"I'm sure," I tell him before he can ask me again.

He sighs but nods as he turns the tattoo gun on and starts to outline her name. We're both quiet while he works and I try to picture Darcy's reaction when she sees it. Maybe I should have warned her before I did this, but I just want to do something to show her how much she means to me, how serious I am about us.

Mischa finishes just before opening and Sam, Nico, and Zeke all come by to get a look and tease me.

"Mischa, I think this might be some of your best work," Zeke says and I look to Mischa.

Judging by the look on his face, he's torn between pride over Zeke's words, and hate because he was the one who tattooed Darcy's name on me. He slaps the bandage over it, making sure to press down just enough that I hiss out a breath at him. He grins smugly at me, and I know that we're even. I tugged my shirt back on and headed up front, greeting my first client of the day.

Now, we're almost done for the day and I glance at the clock to see that it's almost closing time. My schedule says that I still have one last appointment and I forgot to ask Sam about it before she left for the day. I'm assuming that it was some kind of leftover error with the old scheduling system but now I'm stuck waiting to see if anyone shows up.

Darcy and I have been dating again for three weeks and it's been heaven. We're back to texting every day but now we spend more time together face to face too. I spend my days off hanging out at her greenhouse with her and she stops by the shop after work a couple of times a week and hangs out with me while I work. We spend every single night together, taking turns at each other's place.

Things have been perfect and I know that I'm ready to take the next step and tell her how I feel. The words have been on the tip of my tongue ever since we got back together but I've held back. She's just started trusting me and I don't want to mess anything up by pushing her too hard, too fast.

"Hey, lover boy, we're heading out. Are you all good here?" Mischa asks me as he pokes his head into my room.

"Yeah, I'm getting ready to head out too."

"You staying at our place or with Darcy tonight?" he asks me.

He's always keeping track of where I'm sleeping and at first, I thought that it was to give me more shit, but now I'm not so sure. The last couple of times that Darcy has slept over at our place, I'm pretty sure he hasn't been home. I have a feeling that I know where he's been but I've been so focused on Darcy that I haven't had time to ask him what's going on between him and Indie.

"We're sleeping at our place tonight," I tell him and I watch his eyes spark with excitement. "You going to stay with Indie?" I ask casually and I'm surprised when he turns away.

"I don't know. We'll see."

"What's going on with you two anyway?"

"We're just hanging out. Having some fun, ya know? Well, not you 'cause now you're all about the love..." he tries to tease me.

I smirk at him as he straightens and gets ready to leave.

"One day, Mischa. One day you'll meet your match too."

He laughs and flips me off before he heads for the door, yelling goodbye as he goes. I glance at the clock and see it's ten to nine. It doesn't look like any more customers are going to show up so I start to gather my things, picking up my phone and sending a quick text to Darcy that I'll be heading to pick her up in a few minutes. I hit send and then freeze when I hear a phone ding behind me. I didn't hear anyone come in when Mischa left, and I wonder if he left his phone here.

I spin around and my eyes widen when I see Darcy standing there. She's wearing a pair of high heels with a skin tight bandage dress that shows off all of her curves. My mouth waters at the sight and my cock hardens painfully in my jeans as she takes a step toward me.

"Surprise," she says as she steps further into the room.

"I love this surprise," I mumble, still struck dumb by seeing all of Darcy's curves displayed like this. "This is the best surprise ever."

"I have one more surprise for you actually," she says as a blush stains her cheeks.

My cock presses against my zipper, knowing what he wishes the other surprise was. I'm glued to the floor as Darcy walks closer to me, stopping a few feet away and reaching behind her to unzip her dress. She slips it down her arms and wiggles until it drops to pool at her feet.

I groan when I see what she's wearing under her dress. She looks like a 50s pin-up model in her black and white polka dot lingerie. There's a red bow on the bra right between her breasts and another smaller bow on her panties, right over her pussy. I'm dying to take both off with my teeth. I've never thought about having sex in the shop before but now it's all I can picture. To bend her over my table and take her from behind or to lay her out flat on it so that her legs are hanging over the edge. Maybe she could ride me after... my mind flashes with all of the different positions we could try out.

Darcy's thick thighs shift and her hands ball into fists. I look back to her face and notice that she's blushing and looking anywhere but at me, and I realize that she's nervous. She actually seems almost embarrassed but that can't be right. Doesn't she know what she does to me? I get hard just from smelling her perfume or seeing her walk into a room.

"I want you," she says quietly and my hands reach out to her, pulling her flush against me.

She gasps when my erection digs into her soft stomach and I grin down at her.

"You're the hottest thing that I've ever seen in my life."

She blushes and looks away.

"I love you, Darcy. ALL of you."

She blinks up at me, her mouth falling open and I realize that I just told her that I loved her.

"I love you, too."

I grip her tighter, lowering my mouth down as she rises up on her tiptoes to kiss me. Our mouths move slowly over each other, both of us wanting to take our time and enjoy this moment.

I turn us and steer her over until her thighs hit the edge of the table. I grip her hips and lift her up until she's sitting on the edge of the table. My hands stroke up her soft skin until I'm cupping her face. I pull my lips away from hers and stare down at her flushed face.

Her hands tug at my shirt and I realize that I'm still fully dressed. I help her pull it off, forgetting about the tattoo until I've tossed my shirt to the floor. Darcy's eyes lock on the white bandage and my stomach tightens as I wonder how she's going to take my newest tattoo.

"Mischa gave me some new ink this morning."

"Can I see it?"

I nod at her, reaching for the edge of the bandage and slowly pulling it off. Her eyes lock on the red and black writing and she gasps, her mouth forming a perfect O when she sees her name tattooed above my heart. Her eyes are wide as she looks up into mine.

"I love you. You're it for me, Darcy, and I wanted to show you how sure I am of that."

Her eyes get glassy with unshed tears but she smiles at me, wrapping her arms around my neck.

"I love you too, Atlas."

She nods up at me, trust and love shining in her eyes. I brush my lips over hers in a gentle caress, trailing more kisses down her neck and over her clavicle. My hands skim down her back, finding the clasp to her bra and flicking it open. Her lush tits spill out as I slide the straps down her arms and toss the bra to the side. I cup the heavy mounds, finding her sensitive nipples and rolling them between two fingers. She gasps as I continue to tease the stiff peaks.

My lips trail down her delicate skin until I capture one nipple in my mouth. I roll the stiff bud over my tongue, flicking it as my fingers work on her other nipple. Darcy is gasping and moaning as I continue to use my mouth and hands to bring her pleasure. I take turns, licking and pinching each nipple until she starts to tip backward on the table.

I help her lie down and kiss a line down her stomach to the edge of her lace panties. My fingers hook into the sides and I slowly tug them down her creamy thighs until they fall on the floor at my feet. She starts to cover up but I don't want her to feel self-conscious. I want her to be lost in the pleasure so I hurry to get my face back between her thighs.

I lick along her folds the way I know she likes, circling her clit slowly until her hips are rocking against my mouth. I slip one finger inside her snug channel and rub against that spot inside of her that drives her wild. She reaches down, gripping my hair and holding me to her pussy as she comes against my mouth.

I drink her down and we both pant as we try to catch

our breath, our eyes locked on each other. My mind flips to what position we could do in this shop and I decide to play out one fantasy that I've had since the moment that I saw her.

I pull her off the tattoo chair, spinning her around and bending her over my table until her chest is lying flat on the surface. In her heels, she is the perfect height for me to fuck her this way. Her legs spread in invitation and I waste no time in thrusting into her from behind. She moans, her arms bracing against the table as I grip her hips and pound into her. My piercing drags over her g-spot and Darcy screams in pleasure.

She looks over her shoulder at me and our eyes lock. Seeing the passion on her face drives my own lust higher and I can feel my balls draw up closer to my body as my orgasm starts to brew. My pace starts to falter and Darcy's eyes screw shut as her pussy clamps down around my length. She buries her face in the tattoo table and cries out my name as she cums. I shout her name as I follow her and my release fills her waiting womb.

I pull out of her slowly, helping her stand and find her balance in her high heels. I try to catch my breath as I take in her curvy body, debating if I should spread her out on the table again or if I should take her home and make love to her in my bed. It's quiet in the room, in the shop, as I try to think through my options and Darcy seems to take my silence as second thoughts and she starts to cross her arms, doing her best to cover herself up with her arms.

"None of that. I love looking at you. You're perfect."

Her hands slowly drop but I can see the lust and passion slowly disappearing from her eyes as her doubts creep in. I wish that I could make her see her the way that I see her, the way that she really is. An idea hits me then and

I grab her hand, dragging her off the table and out of the room after me. She teeters in her high heels and I slow my pace slightly as I lead her to the back of the shop.

We stop outside the back office, in the center of the mirrors and my dick hardens at the sight, ready for another round. My hands land on her shoulders and I spin her around, forcing her to look in the mirror at us.

"Look at yourself," I whisper in her ear when I notice that she's closed her eyes, trying to block out the sight.

"Come on, Darcy. Do it for me?" I plead and she sighs.

She reluctantly opens her eyes, her gaze wary and sad as she stares at herself in the mirrors before us. I try to comfort her as she stares at her reflection, my hands running down her arms slowly.

"How can you not like what you see? How can you not see how beautiful you are? You have me hard constantly with all these sexy curves. I love your body," I whisper lowly in her ear before I nip her earlobe.

My hot breath washes over her neck and she lets her head drop to the side, giving me more room to work. I take the opportunity and trail a line of hot kisses down the sensitive skin there. My hands trace over her silky skin and she leans back into me as she watches our reflection in the mirror.

"Do you like watching, Darcy?"

Her eyes darken and she bites her full bottom lip, nodding slightly as my hands move from her arms, up her ribcage until I'm cupping her heavy tits in my palms. My thumbs trail over her stiff nipples and her head rolls against my shoulder as I pinch the tight peaks.

"This body is heaven. A real work of art, Darcy. I hate that you can't see that," I say as my eyes meet hers in the mirror. She looks uncertain but her eyes are dark, filled with heat for what I'm doing to her delectable body. I bend my head, biting her shoulder lightly as I pinch her nipples and she gasps, the sound music to my ears.

"I'm going to make you see yourself for who you really are, Darcy. We'll start slow, but soon you're going to love this body as much as I do."

She nods her head against my shoulder, her eyes locked on us in the mirror. My left hand drifts lower over her round stomach until I'm tickling her waistline.

"Look at how well you're doing already. Look at how open you're already being with me."

My erection presses between her ass cheeks as she grinds against me and I slip my hand lower, spreading her lips until her pretty clit pokes out. Her legs shift, spreading wider as I lean down and kiss along her shoulder, my eyes staying locked on her in the mirror. I can see my cum starting to run down her leg and I can't wait any longer.

"Put your hands flat against the mirror. I don't want you hiding any of yourself from me. I want you to watch while I love you."

Her eyes darken more and she takes a step forward, bracing her palms against the mirror as she watches me move around behind her. I grip her hips and pull her ass back toward me so that she's bent forward slightly. I smooth my hands down her back and watch her in the mirror. As soon as her eyes dart away from her reflection, I spank her, my hand slapping down against her round ass.

"Watch what I do to you. Watch what this sexy body does to me."

She nods, her eyes round as she watches my face in the mirror. Her heels put her at the right height so I don't have to bend my knees too much to line up with her dripping opening. I grip my cock, teasing her with the tip as I watch her.

"I don't know how you miss all those other guys always checking you out. Don't worry, I won't let them touch what's mine. Everyone can see how gorgeous you are, Darcy. It's time you do too."

I grip her hips, slamming home inside of her. Her tits bounce with the motion and we both groan as I sink home.

I start up a steady pace, keeping my eyes locked on her in the mirror. Her face is flushed and her hair is a tangled mess around her face but fuck, she still looks so fucking hot.

"Do you see how hot you are? How sexy your body is? You're a goddess, Darcy. One look at you and I was hooked."

She watches me as I continue to fuck her, her fingers gripping the frame around the mirror as she tries to hold herself up. Her eyes are locked on the image of the two of us in the mirror and I can feel her pussy starting to clamp down around my length already. My eyes drift lower and I moan as I watch my cock sliding in and out of her, covered in our juices. I've never had sex where I watched myself before but it seems to be my thing. Both of our thing, if Darcy's flushed appearance and lust-filled eyes are any indication. My fingers dig into her hips and I can't hold my orgasm back anymore. I chant her name as I let go, pounding into her at a frenzied pace as we both reach our peaks.

I catch her, holding her up as she shouts my name, her eyes locked on mine in the mirror as she cums all over my cock. Her juices coat my length and I shout her name as I cum deep inside her once again.

We watch each other silently as I slowly pull out of her and help her gain her balance in her shoes. She catches me off guard when she suddenly spins and throws her arms around my neck, hugging me tightly.

"Thank you," she whispers against my chest.

"I feel like I should be saying that," I joke and she laughs against me.

"For making me feel beautiful, Atlas. You always manage to do that."

I cup her cheek and tilt her face up to mine.

"You're gorgeous, Darcy. I'm going to prove it to you every day until you can finally see what I do, what the world does."

She nods up at me, tears shimmering in her eyes.

"Take me home?"

"Anything for you, Darcy."

TWENTY-TWO

Darcy

I ROLL over in Atlas's bed the next morning and moan at the soreness between my legs. Muscles that I didn't even know I had ache from all of the exertion last night. I close my eyes, a small smile curving my lips as I remember everything that happened between us last night, everything that Atlas did to me. I can feel the familiar pull in my lower belly as I remember the things that he had said to me last night as I watched him fuck me in the mirror.

I'm pulled out of my daydreams when the bed shifts next to me. I blink open my eyes and roll onto my side as Atlas leans up on one elbow and smiles sleepily down at me.

"Mornin'," he says, his voice rough with sleep.

"Good morning."

"How are you feeling?"

"A little sore," I admit, my fingers tracing the lines of a phoenix tattoo on his bicep.

"I guess round two is out of the question until you recover a little bit, huh?"

"I think we had round two last night... and three and four," I say with a giggle as he buries his face in my neck.

"Okay, so no round five then. How about breakfast?"

My stomach growls at the thought and Atlas kisses me quickly before he rolls out of bed. I admire his toned ass as he moves around the room, pulling on some boxers and jeans before he tosses me a pair of sweatpants and a shirt.

"I really need to start keeping some of my things here," I say as I pull his shirt over my head.

It's tight across my chest, the logo stretching over my breasts, and I look up to see Atlas staring, his eyes filled with heat. My mind flashes back to last night in the tattoo shop and I look up to the ceiling.

"You know, I bet you could hang a pretty decent size mirror up there," I say, pointing directly above the bed.

He follows my finger and grins at me, pulling me into his arms.

"Fuck, you have the best ideas."

I laugh against his chest, grabbing his hand and leading him out to the kitchen. I open the fridge, digging out some milk before I find the cereal. He grabs us two bowls and spoons and turns to face me as I pour some Cheerios into my bowl.

"So, about this clothes thing..."

I look at him, confused for a minute before I remember my comment in the bedroom.

"Yeah."

"What if you moved all of your stuff here?"

"Moved in with you, you mean?" I ask, staring at him wide-eyed.

"Yeah. Well, with Mischa, maybe we should get our

own place. More privacy that way. Just think about it, okay? I know it's fast but I'm ready for more. We already spend every single night together and this way we could be together for all of our free time too."

I stare at him, wondering if he's crazy, wondering if I'm crazy for considering it.

"Okay, let's do it. Get our own place."

"Yeah?" he asks, excitement taking over his face.

"Yeah, but I want to talk to Indie about it first and make sure she's okay with me moving out. You should probably make sure Mischa is okay with you moving out too."

"Deal," he says quickly, pulling me in for a tight hug.

We eat our cereal quickly before he hops in the shower and I pack my bag, shoving the dress and heels into my purse and pulling my shoes on.

Atlas drives me back to my place and kisses me good-bye, promising to text me later. I know that he'll talk to Mischa about me moving in at work and I need to talk to Indie. I have a feeling Atlas isn't going to stop pushing until he has all of my stuff over at their apartment.

I head upstairs and open the apartment door, coming up short when I see Mischa standing shirtless in our living room.

"Hey," I say, looking around for Indie.

She comes down the hallway a second later, dressed with a towel wrapped around her hair.

"Hey!" she calls out as she heads to grab a glass of orange juice from the kitchen.

"I'm just headed out. I'll see you guys later," Mischa says as he tugs his shirt on and heads out the door.

I stare after him for a minute before I turn back to my best friend.

"What's going on with you and Mischa?"

Indie blushes, taking a big swig of orange juice to stall for time.

"We're friends... and a little bit more."

"And you're... you're okay with that?" I ask, surprised because Indie has always been a relationship sort of girl.

"Yeah, it's cool, Darcy. I like him a lot. He's just got some hang-ups about relationships and stuff, but I'm okay."

She looks away from me, and I can already tell that she's fallen for him.

"Just... don't let him hurt you, okay? I don't want to have to kick his ass."

She smiles at me and comes to give me a quick hug.

"So, enough about me. How was last night?" she asks, plopping down on the couch.

I sit down next to her, telling her about showing up and surprising him and then the sex. She gets excited when I tell her how good it was and how sore I was this morning and awes when I tell her that we said I love you to each other. I bite my lip as I say the next part.

"He asked me to move in with him."

"OMG, Darcy! That's great. I'm so happy for you two. You deserve a good guy like Atlas."

"You're not mad that I would be leaving you?"

"No! We'll still see each other all of the time and it's not like you're moving that far away. I'm so happy for you guys."

She hugs me again and we hold each other for a minute before we pull away and cuddle on the couch together.

"I'm going to miss living with you," I whisper and she nods against my head.

"Me too, but this is good, Darcy."

"Guess I should start packing," I say after a minute and Indie giggles next to me.

"I'll help. We can make a party out of it."

I smile as I follow her down the hall and into my room.

TWENTY-THREE

Atlas

MISCHA, Nico, Sam, and Zeke help me carry in the last of the boxes from the moving van. Darcy didn't have that much and with all of us helping out, we were able to get everything loaded and moved in one morning before the shop opened. They'll all have to go to work after this but I promised them breakfast burritos for helping. Darcy and Indie just left to pick up the food and I know that they should be back any minute.

"Phew," Mischa says as he puts the last box in my bedroom.

I had asked Mischa if it was okay for her to move in with us and he promised he was cool with it. He had said that he figured it was going to happen sooner or later and he was happy for me. He also added that he didn't think we would be roommates for too much longer. He figured we would get our own place once we got married.

It turns out that an apartment on the next floor down

will be available next month and Darcy and I have already put our deposit down. Darcy and I were going to leave most of her things in boxes but I think that we'll have to unpack some stuff today just so that we can actually move in here. There are boxes stacked up against one wall and more bags thrown on the bed.

I'm glad that Mischa wasn't upset and that everyone gets how much Darcy means to me. These guys are the family that I wish I had. Speaking of my family, I should probably call them soon and tell them about Darcy and our new living situation. I sigh just thinking about making that phone call and decide that it can wait until later.

"Thanks for all the help, guys. We really appreciate it."

Nico just nods before he heads out to the living room and Zeke slaps me on the shoulder. "Anytime, man," he says as he trails after Nico. Sam gives me a side hug before she follows them out to the living room to wait on the food, leaving just me and Mischa alone.

He's staring off into space, something I've seen him do a lot the last day or two. He seems a little off, like something happened but he hasn't brought anything up to me.

"You okay, Misch?" I ask quietly as I hang some of Darcy's clothes up next to mine in the closet.

He doesn't answer me right away and I turn to watch him as he bites on his bottom lip.

"How did you know that Darcy was the one for you?" he asks slowly and I swear my jaw just about hits the floor. I want to tease him and give him shit like he has been doing to me for the past couple of months but he looks kind of down, so I decide to let it slide.

"I just knew when I saw her. She's smart and talented but so kind and compassionate and strong too. A lot of the girls we meet at the shop are... one dimensional? They only seem to care about their looks or their image, you know? How many followers they have and the newest Instagram filter and bullshit like that. None of that interests me. Darcy is different. She just makes me happy. I know it happened fast, but even from the beginning, she was the first person I would think about when I woke up and the last thing I would think about before I fell asleep at night. When she wasn't talking to me, it felt like death. Worse than death. I've never cared if any other girl blew me off but I cared with Darcy. Oh, and the sex is out of this world. I mean the—"

"WHOA! Don't need to know that," Mischa says, holding his hands out to stop me from continuing.

I knew that would get him and I smirk as I hang up some more of Darcy's clothes in the closet next to mine.

"She was just different. I think sometimes you just meet someone and then BAM! There's just chemistry or something and you know that they're the one for you."

He nods when I finish my speech and looks thoughtful. I watch him for a minute before I ask my own question.

"Is this about Indie?" I ask, right as the front door opens and Darcy and Indie call out that the food is here.

"Thank god, I'm starving," Mischa says, dodging my question.

He shoots me a smile that doesn't quite reach his eyes and I know that I was right. He turns and heads toward the kitchen before I can ask him any more about her and him, and I frown as I watch him go. I should have asked him a long time ago what was going on between him and Indie, and guilt hits me. I was so wrapped up in Darcy that I've been neglecting him. I've been a bad friend, but I promise myself that I'll reach out to Mischa soon and get to the bottom of this, to whatever the heck is going on between him and Indie.

I've noticed that Indie seems to be avoiding him today. When we first got to their apartment, Indie had stayed in Darcy's room, helping her pack the last of the boxes. I hadn't thought too much about it at the time but then when Darcy offered to go grab the breakfast burritos, Indie couldn't offer to go with her fast enough. She had practically dragged Darcy out the door and Mischa had looked upset as he watched them go. I hope that they figure out whatever is going on with them because Mischa has seemed happier these last few weeks than in the last two years that I've known him and I know that Indie is the best thing that's ever happened to him.

I hang the last of Darcy's clothes in the closet before I turn to grab some food. Darcy is standing in the doorway watching me.

"It looks pretty cramped in here," she says, taking in all of the boxes.

"We'll get it unpacked and put away fast," I promise her as I walk over and wrap my arms around her waist.

"I'm glad you're here," I whisper as I lower my lips toward hers.

"I am too. I love you, Atlas."

"I love you too," I say as my lips claim hers.

We don't get to get too lost in each other though before someone clears their throat out in the hallway. I pull away from Darcy reluctantly and take her hand in mine, leading her out to the kitchen so that we can eat breakfast with our friends.

We laugh over messy breakfast burritos and weak coffee and I smile, feeling happier than ever now that Darcy is here with me. I know that she's going to be mine forever but

I won't push for more just yet. I pat the ring in my pocket as we say goodbye to everyone and head back to the bedroom to start unpacking.

Soon she'll have my ring on her finger and we'll have our happily ever after. Just like Darcy deserves.

TWENTY-FOUR

Darcy

FIVE YEARS LATER...

I GRIP Atlas's hand tighter as we walk our black and white mutt, Noodles, down the icy sidewalk. He was a stray dog that kept hanging around the nursery. It probably didn't help that I kept feeding him and after the third day of him trailing after me, following me everywhere, I took him home. Atlas hadn't even blinked an eye when I walked in the door with this ball of fur. He had helped me give him a bath before he ran to the store for dog food, toys, and treats. He said I couldn't keep feeding him spaghetti noodles, which is how he got his name.

Atlas rubs his hand over my swollen stomach as we stop to let Noodles pee, and I smile up at him. I'm seven months pregnant with our first baby, a boy that we're going to name

Harvey, and Atlas has been hovering over me, nervous about me getting stressed or lifting anything heavier than a pillow. He even tried to convince me to stay home and let him take Noodles out. He said the roads were too slick and wanted me to stay at our place while he took Noodles for his walk, but I've been cooped up inside all day and I needed to stretch my legs and breathe some fresh air.

Atlas proposed six months after we moved in together and we got married two months later. His parents couldn't make it up for the ceremony, too much work to get done they had said, and even now, five years later, I've only met them once. They weren't mean, just kind of cold and disinterested in their son and his new marital status didn't seem to do anything to change that. They both kind of looked down on him and his friends because of their lifestyle choices and tattoos and when I told them that I owned a greenhouse and landscaping business they had seemed unimpressed. I guess "playing in the dirt" as they had put it, wasn't as cool as being a lawyer like them. They're still wrapped up in their law careers and it makes me sad to think about their lack of a relationship with their son. We stopped trying to see them or spend time with them and I think both of us are happier here in Pittsburgh with the family that we built ourselves.

Atlas tugs me closer into his side as the wind picks up and I can feel how anxious he is to get me back inside our apartment. Mischa is still in the building and it's nice being so close to him. It seems we don't go more than a day without popping in to see each other. It's nice being closer to work now too and since the tattoo shop is on the way home, I can stop and see Atlas at work whenever I like.

Our new apartment is bigger, with plenty of room for

the baby. We've been working on making it ours for the past couple of years. I built our own little private garden on the fire escape, filling the small space with potted plants, and Atlas and I decorated the rest of the place together. Atlas had hung a mirror on our ceiling first thing and I had laughed at that but honestly, I love it. I love watching him move in and out of me, seeing him cage me in with his body as he thrusts into me, or watching his head move between my legs as he eats me out.

I'm not sure if it was the mirror or Atlas or just that I matured, but I've actually gotten to a place where I like my body. I know that I'll never be a size two, and honestly, I'm okay with that. Walking to work has helped me lose some weight and the exercise has given me more energy. I know that Atlas and Indie love the progress that I've made and I know that they were both worried that I would relapse when we found out that I was pregnant but I've been good. I love carrying our son, feeling him grow and move inside of me, and I know that Atlas will love me no matter what.

We've been working on decorating the nursery ever since we found out we were having a boy. Atlas drew a whole mural on one wall and he's going to write his name over the crib in a cool design... just as soon as we can agree on a name.

Our little boy moves inside my belly, kicking and stretching, and I smile as I place my hand against the round bump to feel him kick. I can't wait for him to get here. I never gave much thought to being a mother, too preoccupied with starting my own business, but now that he's almost here, I'm so excited. I can't wait to be a mother, and I know that Atlas is going to be the best father. We both know the type of parents that we don't want to be and I know that

I'll never have to worry about Atlas putting work before his family.

Atlas still works at the shop with Mischa, Nico, and Sam. Zeke still owns it, but he's been there less ever since he got married himself. We still see him and his wife a couple of times a month though when we get together for dinners and brunches.

My business has really taken off, especially after I got the landscaping job from Zeke's friend, Maxwell. I've redone all of his restaurants over the past couple of years and gotten more business than I could handle after that. I've hired more people and let them take over more at both the nursery and landscaping business so that I could spend more time with Atlas and get ready for our new addition.

We make it back to our building and I grin at Atlas as he helps me up the front steps and ushers me inside. He bends down to unleash Noodles, tossing him a treat before he hangs up the leash by the front door. I don't know what I did to deserve this man but I'm thankful every day that I met him and that he fought for us when I was too afraid to follow my heart. Because of him, I have a family, a home, and more self-confidence than ever before.

"Nap time?" he asks me as he helps me take off my coat.

"Actually, I'm in the mood for something else," I say, turning to him with a wink.

He grins down at me, wrapping his arms around my growing waist.

"Anything for you, Darcy."

His lips seal over mine then and I sigh as I lean against him, getting lost in his kiss and in him, just like I always do. I don't know what else our future holds for us but I do know that as long as I have Atlas by my side, we'll be just fine.

WANT MORE EYE CANDY INK? **Then be sure to check out the complete series here!**

YOU CAN ALSO READ **Eye Candy Ink: The Second Generation Here!**

ABOUT THE AUTHOR

CONNECT WITH ME!

If you enjoyed this story, please consider leaving a review on Amazon or any other reader site or blog that you like. Don't forget to recommend it to your other reader friends.

If you want to chat with me, please consider joining my VIP list or connecting with me on one of my Social Media platforms. I love talking with each of my readers. Links below!

Website
Newsletter

Screwed

Fallen Peak

A Very Mountain Man Valentine's Day

A Very Mountain Man Halloween

A Very Mountain Man Thanksgiving

A Very Mountain Man Christmas

A Very Mountain Man New Year

Folklore

Kidnapping His Forever

Claiming His Forever

Finding His Forever

Rescuing His Forever

Chasing His Forever

Folklore: The Complete Series

Holiday Hearts

Be Mine

Falling in Love

Holly Jolly Holidays

Honey Peak

The Trouble With Falling

Love Notes

Signing Off With Love

Care Package Love

Wrong Number, Right Love

Kings Gym

Fighting Fire With Fire

Fighting Tooth and Nail

Fighting Back From Hell

Mine To

Mine to Love

Mine to Protect

Mine to Cherish

Mine to Keep

Sequoia: Stud Farm

Branded

Bucked

Roped

Spurred

Sequoia: Fast Love Racing

Jump Start

Pit Stop

Home Stretch

Telltale Heart

Bought and Paid For

His Miracle

Pretty Girl

Telltale Hearts Boxset

ALSO BY SHAW HART

Still in the mood for Christmas books?

Stuffing Her Stocking, Mistletoe Kisses, Snowed in For Christmas, Coming Down Her Chimney

Love holiday books? Check out these!

For Better or Worse, Riding His Broomstick, Thankful for His FAKE Girlfriend, His New Year Resolution, Hop Stuff, Taming Her Beast, Hungry For Dash, His Firework

Looking for some OTT love stories?

Her Scottish Savior, Baby Mama, Tempted By My Roommate, Blame It On The Rum, Wild Ride, Always

Looking for a celebrity love story?

Bedroom Eyes, Seducing Archer, Finding Their Rhythm

In the mood for some young love books?

Study Dates, His Forever, My Girl

Some other books by Shaw:

The Billionaire's Bet, Her Guardian Angel, Falling Again, Stealing Her, Dreamboat, Making Her His, Trouble

Printed in Great Britain
by Amazon